U0063711

A. de Saint-Exupéry 著

Richard Howard   周克希 譯

THE LITTLE PRINCE

小王子

商務印書館

The Little Prince by Antoine de Saint-Exupéry and translated into the
English language by Richard Howard
English translation copyright ©2000 by Richard Howard

本書譯文由上海世紀出版股份有限公司譯文出版社授權使用

書　　名：*The Little Prince* 小王子

作　　者：A. de Saint-Exupéry

插　　圖：A. de Saint-Exupéry

譯　　者：Richard Howard　　周克希

責任編輯：張朗欣　黃家麗

封面設計：楊愛文

出　　版：商務印書館（香港）有限公司
　　　　　香港筲箕灣耀興道 3 號東滙廣場 8 樓
　　　　　http://www.commercialpress.com.hk

發　　行：香港聯合書刊物流有限公司
　　　　　香港新界荃灣德士古道 220-248 號荃灣工業中心 16 樓

印　　刷：中華商務彩色印刷有限公司
　　　　　香港新界大埔汀麗路 36 號中華商務印刷大廈

版　　次：2022 年 12 月第 1 版第 5 次印刷
　　　　　© 2015 商務印書館（香港）有限公司
　　　　　ISBN 978 962 07 0397 3
　　　　　Printed in Hong Kong

Publisher's Note 出版説明

"只有用心才能看見。"這是狐狸告訴小王子的秘密。在各個星球不同的人，如愛下命令的國王、愛受崇拜的虛榮者、借醉忘羞的酒鬼、迷信數字的商人、忠於職守的點燈人、閉門造車的地理學家等，他們雖然遇上小王子，卻看不見甚麼，惟獨機師見過小王子後判若兩人，箇中原因值得讀者思考。

初、中級英語程度讀者使用本書時，先閱讀英文原文，如遇到理解障礙，則參照中譯作為輔助。在英文原文結束之前或附註解，標註古英語、非現代詞彙拼寫形式及語法；同樣，在譯文結束之前或會附註釋，以幫助讀者理解原文故事背景。如有餘力，讀者可在閱讀原文部份段落後，查閱相應中譯，觀察同樣詞句在雙語中不同的表達。

小王子和機師相遇，發揮出"秘密"的力量，兩人嚐到真摯的友情，機師重拾純真和夢想。可有想過，有一天遇上小王子的是你？

商務印書館 (香港) 有限公司

編輯出版部

Contents　目錄

Preface to the English Translation

In April 1943, *Le Petit Prince* was published in New York, a year before Antoine de Saint-Exupéry was shot down over the Mediterranean by German reconnaissance planes. The English translation, by Katherine Woods, was copyrighted the same year, and the work was dedicated in that translation to 'the child who became Leon Werth. All grown-ups were once children—although few of them remember it.'

As in the case of contemporaries like Mann and Gide (the latter a great admirer of Saint-Exupéry), new versions of 'canonical' translations raise questions (or at least suspicions) of lese-majesté. A second translator into English of *The Little Prince* accepts the responsibility of such an imputation, for it must be acknowledged that all translations date; certain works never do. A new version of a work fifty-seven years old is entitled and, indeed, is obliged to persist further in the letter of that work. Each decade has its circumlocutions, its compliances; the translator seeks these out, as we see in Ms. Woods's pioneer endeavors, falls back on period makeshifts rather than confronting the often radical outrage of what the author, in his incomparable originality, ventures to say. The translator, it is seen in the fullness of time, so rarely ventures in this fashion, but rather falls back, as I say. It is the peculiar privilege of the next translator, in his own day and age, to sally forth, to be inordinate instead of placating or merely plausible. Time reveals all translation to be paraphrase, and it is in the longing for a standard version of a 'beloved' work that we must begin again, we translators—that we must overtake one another.

Richard Howard

TO LEON WERTH

I ask children to forgive me for dedicating this book to a grown-up. I have a serious excuse: this grown-up is the best friend I have in the world. I have another excuse: this grown-up can understand everything, even books for children. I have a third excuse: he lives in France where he is hungry and cold. He needs to be comforted. If all these excuses are not enough, then I want to dedicate this book to the child whom this grown-up once was. All grown-ups were children first. (But few of them remember it.) So I correct my dedication:

TO LEON WERTH
When he was a little boy

Chapter I

Once when I was six I saw a magnificent picture in a book about the jungle, called True Stories. It showed a boa constrictor swallowing a wild beast. Here is a copy of the picture.

In the book it said: 'Boa constrictors swallow their prey whole, without chewing. Afterward they are no longer able to move, and they sleep during the six months of their digestion.'

In those days I thought a lot about jungle adventures, and eventually managed to make my first drawing, using a coloured pencil. My drawing Number One looked like this:

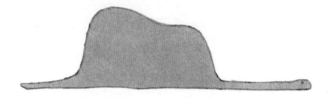

I showed the grown-ups my masterpiece, and I asked them if my drawing scared them.

They answered, 'Why be scared of a hat?'

My drawing was not a picture of a hat. It was a picture of a boa constrictor digesting an elephant. Then I drew the inside of the boa constrictor, so the grown-ups could understand. They always need explanations. My drawing Number Two looked like this:

The grown-ups advised me to put away my drawings of boa constrictors, outside or inside, and apply myself instead to geography, history, arithmetic, and grammar. That is why

I abandoned, at the age of six, a magnificent career as an artist. I had been discouraged by the failure of my drawing Number One and of my drawing Number Two. Grown-ups never understand anything by themselves, and it is exhausting for children to have to provide explanations over and over again.

So then I had to choose another career, and I learned to pilot airplanes. I have flown almost everywhere in the world. And, as a matter of fact, geography has been a big help to me. I could tell China from Arizona at first glance, which is very useful if you get lost during the night.

So I have had, in the course of my life, lots of encounters with lots of serious people. I have spent lots of time with grown-ups. I have seen them at close range... which hasn't much improved my opinion of them.

Whenever I encountered a grown-up who seemed to me at all enlightened, I would experiment on him with my drawing Number One, which I have always kept. I wanted to see if he really understood anything. But he would always answer, 'That's a hat.' Then I wouldn't talk about boa constrictors or jungles or stars. I would put myself on his level and talk about bridge and golf and politics and neckties. And my grown-up was glad to know such a reasonable person.

Chapter II

So I lived all alone, without anyone I could really talk to, until I had to make a crash landing in the Sahara Desert six years ago. Something in my plane's engine had broken, and since I had neither a mechanic nor passengers in the plane with me, I was preparing to undertake the difficult repair job by myself. For me it was a matter of life or death: I had only enough drinking water for eight days.

The first night, then, I went to sleep on the sand a thousand miles from any inhabited country. I was more isolated than a man shipwrecked on a raft in the middle of the ocean. So you can imagine my surprise when I was awakened at daybreak by a funny little voice saying, 'Please... draw me a sheep...'

'What?'

'Draw me a sheep...'

I leaped up as if I had been struck by lightning. I rubbed my eyes hard. I stared. And I saw an extraordinary little fellow staring back at me very seriously. Here is the best portrait I managed to make of him, later on. But of course my drawing is much less attractive than my model. This is not my fault. My career as a painter was discouraged at the age of six by the grown-ups, and I had never learned to draw anything except boa constrictors, outside and inside.

So I stared wide-eyed at this apparition. Don't forget that I was a thousand miles from any inhabited territory. Yet this little fellow seemed to be neither lost nor dying of exhaustion, hunger, or thirst; nor did he seem scared to death. There was nothing in his appearance that suggested a child lost in the middle of the desert a thousand miles from any inhabited territory. When I finally managed to speak, I asked him, 'But... what are you doing here?'

And then he repeated, very slowly and very seriously, 'Please...draw me a sheep...'

In the face of an overpowering mystery, you don't dare disobey. Absurd as it seemed, a thousand miles from all inhabited regions and in danger of death, I took a scrap of paper and a pen out of my pocket. But then I remembered that I had mostly studied geography, history, arithmetic, and grammar, and I told the little fellow (rather crossly) that I didn't know how to draw.

He replied, 'That doesn't matter. Draw me a sheep.'

Since I had never drawn a sheep, I made him one of the only two drawings I knew how to make—the one of the boa constrictor from outside. And I was astounded to hear the little fellow answer:

'No! No! I don't want an elephant inside a boa constrictor. A boa constrictor is very dangerous, and an elephant would get in the way. Where I live, everything is very small. I need a sheep. Draw me a sheep.'

So then I made a drawing.

He looked at it carefully, and then said, 'No. This one is already quite sick. Make another.'

I made another drawing. My friend gave me a kind, indulgent smile:

'You can see for yourself...that's not a sheep, it's a ram. It has horns...'

So I made my third drawing, but it was rejected, like the others:

'This one's too old. I want a sheep that will live a long time.'

So then, impatiently, since I was in a hurry to start work on my engine, I scribbled this drawing, and added, 'This is just the crate. The sheep you want is inside.'

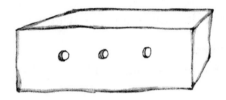

But I was amazed to see my young critic's face light up. 'That's just the kind I wanted! Do you think this sheep will need a lot of grass?'

'Why?'

'Because where I live, everything is very small...'

'There's sure to be enough. I've given you a very small sheep.'

He bent over the drawing. 'Not so small as all that... Look! He's gone to sleep...'

And that's how I made the acquaintance of the little prince.

Chapter III

It took me a long time to understand where he came from. The little prince, who asked me so many questions, never seemed to hear the ones I asked him. It was things he said quite at random that, bit by bit, explained everything. For instance, when he first caught sight of my airplane (I won't draw my airplane; that would be much too complicated for me) he asked:

'What's that thing over there?'

'It's not a thing. It flies. It's an airplane. My airplane.'

And I was proud to tell him I could fly. Then he exclaimed:

'What! You fell out of the sky?'

'Yes,' I said modestly.

'Oh! That's funny...' And the little prince broke into a lovely peal of laughter, which annoyed me a good deal. I like my misfortunes to be taken seriously. Then he added, 'So you fell out of the sky, too. What planet are you from?'

That was when I had the first clue to the mystery of his presence, and I questioned him sharply. 'Do you come from another planet?'

But he made no answer. He shook his head a little, still staring at my airplane. 'Of course, that couldn't have brought you from very far...' And he fell into a reverie that lasted a long while. Then, taking my sheep out of his pocket, he plunged into contemplation of his treasure.

You can imagine how intrigued I was by this hint about 'other planets.' I tried to learn more: 'Where do you come from, little fellow? Where is this 'where I live' of yours? Where will you be taking my sheep?'

After a thoughtful silence he answered, 'The good thing about the crate you've given me is that he can use it for a house after dark.'

'Of course. And if you're good, I'll give you a rope to tie him up during the day. And a stake to tie him to.'

This proposition seemed to shock the little prince.

'Tie him up? What a funny idea!'

'But if you don't tie him up, he'll wander off somewhere

and get lost.'

My friend burst out laughing again. 'Where could he go?'

'Anywhere. Straight ahead...'

Then the little prince remarked quite seriously, 'Even if he did, everything's so small where I live!' And he added, perhaps a little sadly, 'Straight ahead, you can't go very far.'

Chapter IV

That was how I had learned a second very important thing, which was that the planet he came from was hardly bigger than a house!

That couldn't surprise me much. I knew very well that except for the huge planets like Earth, Jupiter, Mars, and Venus, which have been given names, there are hundreds of others that are sometimes so small that it's very difficult to see them through a telescope. When an astronomer discovers one of them, he gives it a number instead of a name. For instance, he would call it 'Asteroid 325.'

I have serious reasons to believe that the planet the little prince came from is Asteroid B-612. This asteroid has been sighted only once by telescope, in 1909 by a Turkish astronomer, who had then made a formal demonstration of his discovery at an International Astronomical Congress. But no one had believed him on account of the way he was dressed. Grown-ups are like that.

Fortunately for the reputation of Asteroid B-612, a Turkish dictator ordered his people, on pain of death, to wear European clothes. The astronomer repeated his demonstration in 1920, wearing a very elegant suit. And this time everyone believed him.

If I've told you these details about Asteroid B-612 and if I've given you its number, it is on account of the grown-ups. Grown-ups like numbers. When you tell them about a new friend, they never ask questions about what really matters. They never ask: 'What does his voice sound like?' 'What games does he like best?' 'Does he collect butterflies?' They ask: 'How old is he?' 'How many brothers does he have?' 'How much does he weigh?' 'How much money does his father make?' Only then do they think they know him. If you tell grown-ups, 'I saw a beautiful red brick house, with geraniums at the windows and doves on the roof...,' they won't be able to imagine such a house. You have to tell them, 'I saw a house worth a hundred thousand francs.' Then they exclaim, 'What a pretty house!'

So if you tell them: 'The proof of the little prince's existence is that he was delightful, that he laughed, and that he wanted a sheep. When someone wants a sheep, that proves he exists,' they shrug their shoulders and treat you like a child! But if you tell them, 'The planet he came from is Asteroid B-612,' then they'll be convinced, and they won't bother you with their questions. That's the way they are. You must not hold it against them. Children should be very understanding of grown-ups.

But, of course, those of us who understand life couldn't care less about numbers! I should have liked to begin this story like a fairy tale. I should have liked to say:

'Once upon a time there was a little prince who lived on a planet hardly any bigger than he was, and who needed a friend...' For those who understand life, that would sound much truer.

The fact is, I don't want my book to be taken lightly. Telling these memories is so painful for me. It's already been six years since my friend went away, taking his sheep with him. If I try to describe him here, it's so I won't forget him. It's sad to forget a friend. Not everyone has had a friend. And I might become like the grown-ups who are no longer interested in anything but numbers. Which is still another reason why I've bought a box of paints and some pencils. It's hard to go back to drawing, at my age, when you've never made any attempts since the one of a boa from inside and the one of a boa from outside, at the age of six! I'll certainly try to make my portraits as true to life as possible. But I'm not entirely sure of succeeding. One drawing works, and the next no longer bears any resemblance. And I'm a little off on his height, too. In this one the little prince is too tall. And here he's too short. And I'm uncertain about the colour of his suit. So I grope in one direction and another, as best I can. In the end, I'm sure to get certain more important details all wrong. But here you'll have to forgive me. My friend never explained anything. Perhaps he thought I was like himself. But I, unfortunately, cannot see a sheep through the sides of a crate. I may be a little like the grown-ups. I must have grown old.

Chapter V

Every day I'd learn something about the little prince's planet, about his departure, about his journey. It would come quite gradually, in the course of his remarks. This was how I learned, on the third day, about the drama of the baobabs.

This time, too, I had the sheep to thank, for suddenly the little prince asked me a question, as if overcome by a grave doubt.

'Isn't it true that sheep eat bushes?'

'Yes, that's right.'

'Ah! I'm glad.'

I didn't understand why it was so important that sheep should eat bushes. But the little prince added:

'And therefore they eat baobabs, too?'

I pointed out to the little prince that baobabs are not

bushes but trees as tall as churches, and that even if he took a whole herd of elephants back to his planet, that herd couldn't finish off a single baobab.

The idea of the herd of elephants made the little prince laugh.

'We'd have to pile them on top of one another.'

But he observed perceptively:

'Before they grow big, baobabs start out by being little.'

'True enough! But why do you want your sheep to eat little baobabs?'

He answered, 'Oh, come on! You know!' as if we were talking about something quite obvious. And I was forced to make a great mental effort to understand this problem all by myself.

And, in fact, on the little prince's planet there were—as on all planets—good plants and bad plants. The good plants come from good seeds, and the bad plants from bad seeds. But the seeds are invisible. They sleep in the secrecy of the ground until one of them decides to wake up. Then it stretches and begins to sprout, quite timidly at first, a charming, harmless little twig reaching toward the sun. If it's a radish seed, or a rosebush seed, you can let it sprout all it likes. But if it's the seed of a bad plant, you must pull the plant up right away, as soon as you can recognize it. As it happens, there were terrible seeds on the little prince's planet...baobab seeds. The planet's soil was infested with them. Now if you attend to a baobab too late, you can never get rid of it again. It overgrows the whole planet. Its roots pierce right through. And if the planet is too small, and if there are too many baobabs, they make it burst into pieces.

'It's a question of discipline,' the little prince told me later on. 'When you've finished washing and dressing each morning, you must tend your planet. You must be sure you pull up the baobabs regularly, as soon as you can tell them apart from the rosebushes, which they closely resemble when they're very young. It's very tedious work, but very easy.'

And one day he advised me to do my best to make a beautiful drawing, for the edification of the children where I live. 'If they travel someday,' he told me, 'it could be useful to them. Sometimes there's no harm in postponing your work until later. But with baobabs, it's always a catastrophe. I knew one planet that was inhabited by a lazy man. He had neglected three bushes...'

So, following the little prince's instructions, I have drawn that planet. I don't much like assuming the tone of a moralist. But the danger of baobabs is so little recognized, and the risks run by anyone who might get lost on an asteroid are so considerable, that for once I am making an exception to my habitual reserve. I say, 'Children, watch out for baobabs!' It's to warn my friends of a danger of which they, like myself, have long been unaware that I worked so hard on this drawing. The lesson I'm teaching is worth the trouble. You may be asking, 'Why are there no other draw-

ings in this book as big as the drawing of the baobabs?'
There's a simple answer: I tried but I couldn't manage it.
When I drew the baobabs, I was inspired by a sense of
urgency.

Chapter VI

O little prince! Gradually, this was how I came to understand your sad little life. For a long time your only entertainment was the pleasure of sunsets. I learned this new detail on the morning of the fourth day, when you told me:

'I really like sunsets. Let's go look at one now...'

'But we have to wait ...'

'What for?'

'For the sun to set.'

At first you seemed quite surprised, and then you laughed at yourself. And you said to me, 'I think I'm still at home!'

Indeed. When it's noon in the United States, the sun, as

everyone knows, is setting over France. If you could fly to France in one minute, you could watch the sunset. Unfortunately France is much too far. But on your tiny planet, all you had to do was move your chair a few feet. And you would watch the twilight whenever you wanted to...

'One day I saw the sunset forty-four times!' And a little later you added, 'You know, when you're feeling very sad, sunsets are wonderful...'

'On the day of the forty-four times, were you feeling very sad?'

But the little prince didn't answer.

Chapter VII

On the fifth day, thanks again to the sheep, another secret of the little prince's life was revealed to me. Abruptly, with no preamble, he asked me, as if it were the fruit of a problem long pondered in silence: 'If a sheep eats bushes, does it eat flowers, too?'

'A sheep eats whatever it finds.'

'Even flowers that have thorns?'

'Yes. Even flowers that have thorns.'

'Then what good are thorns?'

I didn't know. At that moment I was very busy trying to unscrew a bolt that was jammed in my engine. I was quite worried, for my plane crash was beginning to seem extremely serious, and the lack of drinking water made me fear the worst.

'What good are thorns?'

The little prince never let go of a question once he had asked it. I was annoyed by my jammed bolt, and I answered without thinking.

'Thorns are no good for anything—they're just the flowers' way of being mean!'

'Oh!' But after a silence, he lashed out at me, with a sort of bitterness. 'I don't believe you! Flowers are weak. They're naive. They reassure themselves whatever way they can. They believe their thorns make them frightening...'

I made no answer. At that moment I was thinking, *If this bolt stays jammed, I'll knock it off with the hammer.* Again the little prince disturbed my reflections.

'Then you think flowers...'

'No, not at all. I don't think anything! I just said whatever came into my head. I'm busy here with something serious!'

He stared at me, astounded.

' "Something serious"!'

He saw me holding my hammer, my fingers black with grease, bending over an object he regarded as very ugly.

'You talk like the grown-ups!'

That made me a little ashamed. But he added, mercilessly:

'You confuse everything...You've got it all mixed up!' He was really very annoyed. He tossed his golden curls in the wind. 'I know a planet inhabited by a red-faced gentleman. He's never smelled a flower. He's never looked at a star. He's never loved anyone. He's never done anything except add up numbers. And all day long he says over and over, just like you, 'I'm a serious man! I'm a serious man!' And that puffs him up with pride. But he's not a man at all—he's a mushroom!'

'He's a what?'

'A mushroom!' The little prince was now quite pale with rage. 'For millions of years flowers have been producing thorns. For millions of years sheep have been eating them all the same. And it's not serious, trying to understand why flowers go to such trouble to produce thorns that are good for nothing? It's not important, the war between the sheep and the flowers? It's no more serious and more important than the numbers that fat red gentleman is adding up? Suppose I happen to know a unique flower, one that exists nowhere in the world except on my planet, one that a little sheep can wipe out in a single bite one morning, just like that, without even realizing what he's doing—that isn't important?' His face turned red now, and he went on. 'If someone loves a flower of which just one example exists among all the millions and millions of stars, that's enough to make him happy when he looks at the stars. He tells himself, 'My flower's up there somewhere...' But if the sheep eats the flower, then for him it's as if, suddenly, all the stars went out. And that isn't important?'

He couldn't say another word. All of a sudden he burst out sobbing. Night had fallen. I dropped my tools. What did I care about my hammer, about my bolt, about thirst and death? There was, on one star, on one planet, on mine, the Earth, a little prince to be consoled! I took him in my arms. I rocked him. I told him, 'The flower you love is not in danger...I'll draw you a muzzle for your sheep...I'll draw you a fence for your flower...I...' I didn't know what to say. How clumsy I felt! I didn't know how to reach him, where to find him...It's so mysterious, the land of tears.

Chapter VIII

I soon learned to know that flower better. On the little prince's planet, there had always been very simple flowers, decorated with a single row of petals so that they took up no room at all and got in no one's way. They would appear one morning in the grass, and would fade by nightfall. But this one had grown from a seed brought from who knows where, and the little prince had kept a close watch over a sprout that was not like any of the others. It might have been a new kind of baobab. But the sprout soon stopped growing and began to show signs of blossoming. The little prince, who had watched the development of an enormous bud, realized that some sort of miraculous apparition would emerge from it, but the flower continued her beauty preparations in the shelter of her green chamber, selecting her colours with the greatest care and dressing quite deliberately, adjusting her petals one by one. She had no desire to emerge all rumpled, like the poppies. She wished to appear only in the full radiance of her beauty. Oh yes, she was quite vain! And her mysterious adornment had lasted days and days. And then one morning, precisely at sunrise, she showed herself.

And after having laboured so painstakingly, she yawned and said, 'Ah! I'm hardly awake...Forgive me...I'm still all untidy...'

But the little prince couldn't contain his admiration.

'How lovely you are!'

'Aren't I?' the flower answered sweetly. 'And I was born the same time as the sun...'

The little prince realized that she wasn't any too modest, but she was so dazzling!

'I believe it is breakfast time,' she had soon added. 'Would you be so kind as to tend to me?' And the little prince, utterly abashed, having gone to look for a watering can, served the flower.

She had soon begun tormenting him with her rather touchy vanity. One day, for instance, alluding to her four thorns, she remarked to the little prince, 'I'm ready for tigers, with all their claws!'

'There are no tigers on my planet,' the little prince had objected, 'and besides, tigers don't eat weeds.'

'I am not a weed,' the flower sweetly replied.

'Forgive me...'

'I am not at all afraid of tigers, but I have a horror of drafts. You wouldn't happen to have a screen?'

'A horror of drafts...that's not a good sign, for a plant,' the little prince had observed. 'How complicated this flower is...'

'After dark you will put me under glass. How cold it is where you live—quite uncomfortable. Where I come from—' But she suddenly broke off. She had come here as a seed. She couldn't have known anything of other worlds. Humiliated at having let herself be caught on the verge of so naive a lie, she coughed two or three times in order to put the little prince in the wrong. 'That screen?' 'I was going to look for one, but you were speaking to me!' Then she made herself cough again, in order to inflict a twinge of remorse on him all the same.

So the little prince, despite all the goodwill of his love, had soon come to mistrust her. He had taken seriously certain inconsequential remarks and had grown very unhappy.

'I shouldn't have listened to her,' he confided to me one day. 'You must never listen to flowers. You must look at them and smell them. Mine perfumed my planet, but I didn't know how to enjoy that. The business about the tiger claws, instead of annoying me, ought to have moved me...'

And he confided further, 'In those days, I didn't understand anything. I should have judged her according to her actions, not her words. She perfumed my planet and lit up my life. I should never have run away! I ought to have realized the tenderness underlying her silly pretensions. Flowers are so contradictory! But I was too young to know how to love her.'

Chapter IX

In order to make his escape, I believe he took advantage of a migration of wild birds. On the morning of his departure, he put his planet in order. He carefully raked out his active volcanoes. The little prince possessed two active volcanoes, which were very convenient for warming his breakfast. He also possessed one extinct volcano. But, as he said, 'You never know!' So he raked out the extinct volcano, too. If they are properly raked out, volcanoes burn gently and regularly, without eruptions. Volcanic eruptions are like fires in a chimney. Of course, on our Earth we are much too small to rake out our volcanoes. That is why they cause us so much trouble.

The little prince also uprooted, a little sadly, the last

baobab shoots. He believed he would never be coming back. But all these familiar tasks seemed very sweet to him on this last morning. And when he watered the flower one last time, and put her under glass, he felt like crying.

'Good-bye,' he said to the flower.

But she did not answer him.

'Good-bye,' he repeated.

The flower coughed. But not because she had a cold.

'I've been silly,' she told him at last. 'I ask your forgiveness. Try to be happy.'

He was surprised that there were no reproaches. He stood there, quite bewildered, holding the glass bell in midair. He failed to understand this calm sweetness.

'Of course I love you,' the flower told him. 'It was my fault you never knew. It doesn't matter. But you were just as silly as I was. Try to be happy...Put that glass thing down. I don't want it anymore.'

'But the wind...'

'My cold isn't that bad...The night air will do me good. I'm a flower.'

'But the animals...'

'I need to put up with two or three caterpillars if I want to get to know the butterflies. Apparently they're very beautiful. Otherwise who will visit me? You'll be far away. As for the big animals, I'm not afraid of them. I have my own claws.' And she naively showed her four thorns. Then she added, 'Don't hang around like this; it's irritating. You made up your mind to leave. Now go.'

For she didn't want him to see her crying. She was such a proud flower. ...

Chapter X

He happened to be in the vicinity of Asteroids 325, 326, 327, 328, 329, and 330. So he began by visiting them, to keep himself busy and to learn something.

The first one was inhabited by a king. Wearing purple and ermine, he was sitting on a simple yet majestic throne.

'Ah! Here's a subject!' the king exclaimed when he caught sight of the little prince.

And the little prince wondered, *How can he know who I am if he's never seen me before?* He didn't realize that for kings, the world is extremely simplified: All men are subjects.

'Approach the throne so I can get a better look at you,' said the king, very proud of being a king for someone at last.

The little prince looked around for a place to sit down, but the planet was covered by the magnificent ermine cloak. So he remained standing, and since he was tired, he yawned.

'It is a violation of etiquette to yawn in a king's presence,' the monarch told him. 'I forbid you to do so.'

'I can't help it,' answered the little prince, quite embarrassed. 'I've made a long journey, and I haven't had any sleep...'

'Then I command you to yawn,' said the king. 'I haven't seen anyone yawn for years. For me, yawns are a curiosity. Come on, yawn again! It is an order.'

'That intimidates me...I can't do it now,' said the little prince, blushing deeply.

'Well, well!' the king replied. 'Then I...I command you to yawn sometimes and sometimes to...' He was sputtering a little, and seemed annoyed.

For the king insisted that his authority be universally respected. He would tolerate no disobedience, being an absolute monarch. But since he was a kindly[1] man, all his commands were reasonable. 'If I were to command,' he would often say, 'if I were to command a general to turn into a seagull, and if the general did not obey, that would not be the general's fault. It would be mine.'

'May I sit down?' the little prince timidly inquired.

'I command you to sit down,' the king replied, majestically gathering up a fold of his ermine robe.

But the little prince was wondering. The planet was tiny. Over what could the king really reign? 'Sire[2]...,' he ventured, 'excuse me for asking...'

'I command you to ask,' the king hastened to say.

'Sire...over what do you reign?'

'Over everything,' the king answered, with great simplicity.

'Over everything?'

With a discreet gesture the king pointed to his planet, to the other planets, and to the stars.

'Over all that?' asked the little prince.

'Over all that...,' the king answered.

For not only was he an absolute monarch, but a universal monarch as well.

'And do the stars obey you?'

'Of course,' the king replied. 'They obey immediately. I tolerate no insubordination.'

Such power amazed the little prince. If he had wielded it

himself, he could have watched not forty-four but seventy-two, or even a hundred, even two hundred sunsets on the same day without ever having to move his chair! And since he was feeling rather sad on account of remembering his own little planet, which he had forsaken, he ventured to ask a favour of the king: 'I'd like to see a sunset...Do me a favour, your majesty...Command the sun to set...'

'If I commanded a general to fly from one flower to the next like a butterfly, or to write a tragedy, or to turn into a seagull, and if the general did not carry out my command, which of us would be in the wrong, the general or me?'

'You would be,' said the little prince, quite firmly.

'Exactly. One must command from each what each can perform,' the king went on. 'Authority is based first of all upon reason. If you command your subjects to jump in the ocean, there will be a revolution. I am entitled to command obedience because my orders are reasonable.'

'Then my sunset?' insisted the little prince, who never let go of a question once he had asked it.

'You shall have your sunset. I shall command it. But I shall wait, according to my science of government, until conditions are favourable.'

'And when will that be?' inquired the little prince.

'Well, well!' replied the king, first consulting a large

calendar.

'Well, well! That will be around...around...that will be tonight around seven-forty! And you'll see how well I am obeyed.'

The little prince yawned. He was regretting his lost sunset. And besides, he was already growing a little bored. 'I have nothing further to do here,' he told the king. 'I'm going to be on my way!'

'Do not leave!' answered the king, who was so proud of having a subject. 'Do not leave; I shall make you my minister!'

'A minister of what?'

'Of...of justice!'

'But there's no one here to judge!'

'You never know,' the king told him. 'I have not yet explored the whole of my realm. I am very old, I have no room for a carriage, and it wearies me to walk.'

'Oh, but I've already seen for myself,' said the little prince, leaning forward to glance one more time at the other side of the planet. 'There's no one over there, either...'

'Then you shall pass judgment on yourself,' the king answered. 'That is the hardest thing of all. It is much harder to judge yourself than to judge others. If you succeed in judging yourself, it's because you are truly a wise man.'

'But I can judge myself anywhere,' said the little prince. 'I don't need to live here.'

'Well, well!' the king said. 'I have good reason to believe that there is an old rat living somewhere on my planet. I hear him at night. You could judge that old rat. From time to time you will condemn him to death. That way his life will depend on your justice. But you'll pardon him each time for economy's sake. There's only one rat.'

'I don't like condemning anyone to death,' the little prince said, 'and now I think I'll be on my way.'

'No,' said the king.

The little prince, having completed his preparations, had no desire to aggrieve the old monarch. 'If Your Majesty desires to be promptly obeyed, he should give me a reasonable command. He might command me, for instance, to leave before this minute is up. It seems to me that conditions are favourable...'

The king having made no answer, the little prince hesitated at first, and then, with a sigh, took his leave.

'I make you my ambassador,' the king hastily shouted after him. He had a great air of authority.

'Grown-ups are so strange,' the little prince said to himself as he went on his way.

Chapter XI

The second planet was inhabited by a very vain man.
'Ah! A visit from an admirer!' he exclaimed when he caught sight of the little prince, still at some distance. To vain men, other people are admirers.

'Hello,' said the little prince. 'That's a funny hat you're wearing.'

'It's for answering acclamations,' the very vain man replied. 'Unfortunately, no one ever comes this way.'

'Is that so?' said the little prince, who did not understand what the vain man was talking about.

'Clap your hands,' directed the man. The little prince clapped his hands, and the very vain man tipped his hat in modest acknowledgment.

This is more entertaining than the visit to the king, the little prince said to himself. And he continued clapping. The very vain man continued tipping his hat in acknowledgment.

After five minutes of this exercise, the little prince tired of the game's monotony. 'And what would make the hat fall off?' he asked.

But the vain man did not hear him. Vain men never hear anything but praise.

'Do you really admire me a great deal?' he asked the little prince.

'What does that mean—admire?'

'To admire means to acknowledge that I am the handsomest, the best-dressed, the richest, and the most intelligent man on the planet.'

'But you're the only man on your planet!'

'Do me this favour. Admire me all the same.'

'I admire you,' said the little prince, with a little shrug of his shoulders, 'but what is there about my admiration that interests you so much?' And the little prince went on his way.

'Grown-ups are certainly very strange,' he said to himself as he continued on his journey.

Chapter XII

The next planet was inhabited by a drunkard. This visit was a very brief one, but it plunged the little prince into a deep depression.

'What are you doing there?' he asked the drunkard, whom he found sunk in silence before a collection of empty bottles and a collection of full ones.

'Drinking,' replied the drunkard, with a gloomy expression.

'Why are you drinking?' the little prince asked.

'To forget,' replied the drunkard.

'To forget what?' inquired the little prince, who was already feeling sorry for him.

'To forget that I'm ashamed," confessed the drunkard,

hanging his head.

'What are you ashamed of?' inquired the little prince, who wanted to help.

'Of drinking?' concluded the drunkard, withdrawing into silence for good. And the little prince went on his way, puzzled.

'Grown-ups are certainly very, very strange,' he said to himself as he continued on his journey.

Chapter XIII

The fourth planet belonged to a businessman. This person was so busy that he didn't even raise his head when the little prince arrived.

'Hello,' said the little prince. 'Your cigarette's gone out.'

'Three and two make five. Five and seven, twelve. Twelve and three, fifteen. Hello. Fifteen and seven, twenty-two. Twenty-two and six, twenty-eight. No time to light it again. Twenty-six and five, thirty-one. Whew! That amounts to five-hundred-and-one million, six-hundred-twenty-two thousand, seven hundred thirty-one.'

'Five-hundred million what?'

'Hmm? You're still there? Five-hundred-and-one

million...I don't remember...I have so much work to do! I'm a serious man. I can't be bothered with trifles! Two and five, seven...'

'Five-hundred-and-one million what?' repeated the little prince, who had never in his life let go of a question once he had asked it.

The businessman raised his head. 'For the fifty-four years I've inhabited this planet, I've been interrupted only three times. The first time was twenty-two years ago, when I was interrupted by a beetle that had fallen onto my desk from god knows where. It made a terrible noise, and I made four mistakes in my calculations. The second time was eleven years ago, when I was interrupted by a fit of rheumatism. I don't get enough exercise. I haven't time to take strolls. I'm a serious person. The third time...is right now! Where was I? Five-hundred-and-one million...'

'Million what?'

The businessman realized that he had no hope of being left in peace. 'Oh, of those little things you sometimes see in the sky.'

'Flies?'

'No, those little shiny things.'

'Bees?'

'No, those little golden things that make lazy people

daydream. Now, I'm a serious person. I have no time for daydreaming.'

'Ah! You mean the stars?'

'Yes, that's it. Stars.'

'And what do you do with five-hundred million stars?'

'Five-hundred-and-one million, six-hundred-twenty-two thousand, seven hundred thirty-one. I'm a serious person, and I'm accurate.'

'And what do you do with those stars?

'What do I do with them?'

'Yes.'

'Nothing. I own them.'

'You own the stars?'

'Yes.'

'But I've already seen a king who—"

'Kings don't own. They "reign" over...It's quite different.'

'And what good does owning the stars do you?'

'It does me the good of being rich.'

'And what good does it do you to be rich?'

'It lets me buy other stars, if somebody discovers them.'

The little prince said to himself, This man argues a little like my drunkard. Nevertheless he asked more questions. 'How can someone own the stars?'

'To whom do they belong?' retorted the businessman

grumpily.

'I don't know. To nobody."

'Then they belong to me, because I thought of it first.'

'And that's all it takes?'

'Of course. When you find a diamond that belongs to nobody in particular, then it's yours. When you find an island that belongs to nobody in particular, it's yours. When you're the first person to have an idea, you patent it and it's yours. Now I own the stars, since no one before me ever thought of owning them.'

'That's true enough,' the little prince said. 'And what do you do with them?'

'I manage them. I count them and then count them again,' the businessman said. 'It's difficult work. But I'm a serious person!'

The little prince was still not satisfied. 'If I own a scarf, I can tie it around my neck and take it away. If I own a flower, I can pick it and take it away. But you can't pick the stars!'

'No, but I can put them in the bank.'

'What does that mean?'

'That means that I write the number of my stars on a slip of paper. And then I lock that slip of paper in a drawer.'

'And that's all?"

'That's enough!'

That's amusing, thought the little prince. And even poetic. But not very serious. The little prince had very different ideas about serious things from those of the grown-ups. 'I own a flower myself,' he continued, 'which I water every day. I own three volcanoes, which I rake out every week. I even rake out the extinct one. You never know. So it's of some use to my volcanoes, and it's useful to my flower, that I own them. But you're not useful to the stars.'

The businessman opened his mouth but found nothing to say in reply, and the little prince went on his way.

'Grown-ups are certainly quite extraordinary' was all he said to himself as he continued on his journey.

Chapter XIV

The fifth planet was very strange. It was the smallest of all. There was just enough room for a street lamp and a lamplighter. The little prince couldn't quite understand what use a street lamp and a lamplighter could be up there in the sky, on a planet without any people and not a single house. However, he said to himself, *It's quite possible that this man is absurd. But he's less absurd than the king, the very vain man, the businessman, and the drunkard. At least his work has some meaning. When he lights his lamp, it's as if he's bringing one more star to life, or one more flower. When he puts out his lamp, that sends the flower or the star to sleep. Which is a fine occupation. And therefore truly useful.*

When the little prince reached this planet, he greeted the lamplighter respectfully.

'Good morning. Why have you just put out your lamp?'

'Orders,' the lamplighter answered. 'Good morning.'

'What orders are those?'

'To put out my street lamp. Good evening.' And he lit his lamp again.

'But why have you just lit your lamp again?'

'Orders.'

'I don't understand,' said the little prince.

'There's nothing to understand,' said the lamplighter. 'Orders are orders. Good morning.' And he put out his lamp. Then he wiped his forehead with a red-checked[3] handkerchief. 'It's a terrible job I have. It used to be reasonable enough. I put the lamp out mornings and lit it after dark. I had the rest of the day for my own affairs, and the rest of the night for sleeping.'

'And since then orders have changed?'

'Orders haven't changed,' the lamplighter said. 'That's just the trouble! Year by year the planet is turning faster and faster, and orders haven't changed!'

'Which means?'

'Which means that now that the planet revolves once a minute, I don't have an instant's rest. I light my lamp and turn it out once every minute!'

'That's funny! Your days here are one minute long!'

'It's not funny at all,' the lamplighter said. 'You and I have already been talking to each other for a month.'

'A month?'

'Yes. Thirty minutes. Thirty days! Good evening.' And he lit his lamp.

The little prince watched him, growing fonder and fonder of this lamplighter who was so faithful to orders. He remembered certain sunsets that he himself used to follow in other days, merely by shifting his chair. He wanted to help his friend.

'You know...I can show you a way to take a rest whenever you want to.'

'I always want to rest,' the lamplighter said, for it is possible to be faithful and lazy at the same time.

The little prince continued, 'Your planet is so small that you can walk around it in three strides. All you have to do is walk more slowly, and you'll always be in the sun. When you want to take a rest just walk...and the day will last as long as you want it to.'

'What good does that do me,' the lamplighter said, 'when the one thing in life I want to do is sleep?'

'Then you're out of luck,' said the little prince.

'I am,' said the lamplighter. 'Good morning.' And he put out his lamp.

Now that man, the little prince said to himself as he continued on his journey, that man would be despised by all the others, by the king, by the very vain man, by the drunkard, by the businessman. Yet he's the only one who doesn't strike me as ridiculous. Perhaps it's because he's thinking of something besides himself. He heaved a sigh of regret and said to himself, again, That man is the only one I might have made my friend. But his planet is really too small. There's not room for two...

What the little prince dared not admit was that he most regretted leaving that planet because it was blessed with one thousand, four hundred forty sunsets every twenty-four hours!

Chapter XV

The sixth planet was ten times bigger than the last. It was inhabited by an old gentleman who wrote enormous books.

'Ah, here comes an explorer,' he exclaimed when he caught sight of the little prince, who was feeling a little winded and sat down on the desk. He had already travelled so much and so far!

'Where do you come from?' the old gentleman asked him.

'What's that big book?' asked the little prince. 'What do you do with it?'

'I'm a geographer,' the old gentleman answered.

'And what's a geographer?'

'A scholar who knows where the seas are, and the rivers, the cities, the mountains, and the deserts.'

'That is very interesting,' the little prince said. 'Here at last is someone who has a real profession!' And he gazed around him at the geographer's planet. He had never seen a planet so majestic. 'Your planet is very beautiful,' he said. 'Does it have any oceans?'

'I couldn't say,' said the geographer.

'Oh!' The little prince was disappointed. 'And mountains?'

'I couldn't say,' said the geographer.

'And cities and rivers and deserts?'

'I couldn't tell you that, either,' the geographer said.

'But you're a geographer!'

'That's right,' said the geographer, 'but I'm not an explorer. There's not one explorer on my planet. A geographer doesn't go out to describe cities, rivers, mountains, seas, oceans, and deserts. A geographer is too important to go wandering about. He never leaves his study. But he receives the explorers there. He questions them, and he writes down what they remember. And if the memories of one of the explorers seem interesting to him, then the geographer conducts an inquiry into that explorer's moral character.'

'Why is that?'

'Because an explorer who told lies would cause disasters in the geography books, as would an explorer who drank too much.'

'Why is that?' the little prince asked again.

'Because drunkards see double. And the geographer would write down two mountains where there was only one.'

'I know someone,' said the little prince, 'who would be a bad explorer.'

'Possibly. Well, when the explorer's moral character seems to be a good one, an investigation is made into his discovery.'

'By going to see it?'

'No, that would be too complicated. But the explorer is required to furnish proofs. For instance, if he claims to have discovered a large mountain, he is required to bring back large stones from it.' The geographer suddenly grew excited. 'But you come from far away! You're an explorer! You must describe your planet for me!'

And the geographer, having opened his logbook, sharpened his pencil. Explorers' reports are first recorded in pencil; ink is used only after proofs have been furnished.

'Well?' said the geographer expectantly.

'Oh, where I live,' said the little prince, 'is not very interesting. It's so small. I have three volcanoes, two active and one extinct. But you never know.'

'You never know,' said the geographer.

'I also have a flower.'

'We don't record flowers,' the geographer said.

'Why not? It's the prettiest thing!'

'Because flowers are ephemeral.'

'What does ephemeral mean?'

'Geographies,' said the geographer, 'are the finest books of all. They never go out of fashion. It is extremely rare for a mountain to change position. It is extremely rare for an ocean to be drained of its water. We write eternal things.'

'But extinct volcanoes can come back to life,' the little prince interrupted. 'What does ephemeral mean?'

'Whether volcanoes are extinct or active comes down to the same thing for us,' said the geographer. 'For us what counts is the mountain. That doesn't change.'

'But what does ephemeral mean?' repeated the little prince, who had never in all his life let go of a question once he had asked it.

'It means,"which is threatened by imminent disappearance." '

'Is my flower threatened by imminent disappearance?'

'Of course.'

My flower is ephemeral, the little prince said to himself, and she has only four thorns with which to defend herself against the world! And I've left her all alone where I live!

That was his first impulse of regret. But he plucked up his courage again. 'Where would you advise me to visit?' he asked.

'The planet Earth,' the geographer answered. 'It has a good reputation.'

And the little prince went on his way, thinking about his flower.

Chapter XVI

The seventh planet, then, was the Earth.

The Earth is not just another planet! It contains one hundred and eleven kings (including, of course, the African kings), seven thousand geographers, nine-hundred thousand businessmen, seven-and-a-half million drunkards, three-hundred-eleven million vain men; in other words, about two billion grown-ups.

To give you a notion of the Earth's dimensions, I can tell you that before the invention of electricity, it was necessary to maintain, over the whole of six continents, a veritable army of four-hundred-sixty-two thousand, five hundred and eleven lamplighters.

Seen from some distance, this made a splendid effect. The movements of this army were ordered like those of a ballet. First came the turn of the lamplighters of New

Zealand and Australia; then these, having lit their street lamps, would go home to sleep. Next it would be the turn of the lamplighters of China and Siberia to perform their steps in the lamplighters' ballet, and then they too would vanish into the wings. Then came the turn of the lamplighters of Russia and India. Then those of Africa and Europe. Then those of South America, and of North America. And they never missed their cues for their appearances onstage. It was awe-inspiring.

Only the lamplighter of the single street lamp at the North Pole and his colleague of the single street lamp at the South Pole led carefree, idle lives: They worked twice a year.

Chapter XVII

Trying to be witty leads to lying, more or less. What I just told you about the lamplighters isn't completely true, and I risk giving a false idea of our planet to those who don't know it. Men occupy very little space on Earth. If the two billion inhabitants of the globe were to stand close together, as they might for some big public event, they would easily fit into a city block that was twenty miles long and twenty miles wide. You could crowd all humanity onto the smallest Pacific islet.

Grown-ups, of course, won't believe you. They're convinced they take up much more room. They consider themselves as important as the baobabs. So you should advise them to make their own calculations—they love numbers, and they'll enjoy it. But don't waste your time on this extra task. It's unnecessary. Trust me.

So once he reached Earth, the little prince was quite surprised not to see anyone. He was beginning to fear he had come to the wrong planet, when a moon-coloured loop uncoiled on the sand.

'Good evening,' the little prince said, just in case.

'Good evening,' said the snake.

'What planet have I landed on?' asked the little prince.

'On the planet Earth, in Africa,' the snake replied.

'Ah!...And are there no people on Earth?'

'It's the desert here. There are no people in the desert. Earth is very big,' said the snake.

The little prince sat down on a rock and looked up into the sky.

'I wonder,' he said, 'if the stars are lit up so that each of us can find his own, someday. Look at my planet—it's just overhead. But so far away!'

'It's lovely,' the snake said. 'What have you come to Earth for?'

'I'm having difficulties with a flower,' the little prince said.

'Ah!' said the snake.

And they were both silent.

'Where are the people?' The little prince finally resumed the conversation. 'It's a little lonely in the desert...'

'It's also lonely with people,' said the snake.

The little prince looked at the snake for a long time. 'You're a funny creature,' he said at last, 'no thicker than a finger.'

'But I'm more powerful than a king's finger,' the snake said.

The little prince smiled.

'You're not very powerful...You don't even have feet. You couldn't travel very far.'

'I can take you further than a ship,' the snake said. He coiled around the little prince's ankle, like a golden bracelet. 'Anyone I touch, I send back to the land from which he came,' the snake went on. 'But you're innocent, and you come from a star...'

The little prince made no reply.

'I feel sorry for you, being so weak on this granite earth,' said the snake. 'I can help you, someday, if you grow too homesick for your planet. I can—'

'Oh, I understand just what you mean,' said the little prince, 'but why do you always speak in riddles?'

'I solve them all,' said the snake.

And they were both silent.

Chapter XVIII

The little prince crossed the desert and encountered only one flower. A flower with three petals—a flower of no consequence...

'Good morning,' said the little prince.

'Good morning,' said the flower.

'Where are the people?' the little prince inquired politely.

The flower had one day seen a caravan passing.

'People? There are six or seven of them, I believe, in existence. I caught sight of them years ago. But you never know where to find them. The wind blows them away. They have no roots, which hampers them a good deal.'

'Good-bye,' said the little prince.

'Good-bye,' said the flower.

Chapter XIX

The little prince climbed a high mountain. The only mountains he had ever known were the three volcanoes, which came up to his knee. And he used the extinct volcano as a footstool. *From a mountain as high as this one, he said to himself, I'll get a view of the whole planet and all the people on it...*But he saw nothing but rocky peaks as sharp as needles.

'Hello,' he said, just in case.

'Hello...hello...hello...,' the echo answered.

'Who are you?' asked the little prince.

'Who are you... who are you... who are you...,' the echo answered.

'Let's be friends. I am lonely,' he said.

'I am lonely...I am lonely...I am lonely...,' the echo answered.

What a peculiar planet! he thought. It's all dry and sharp and hard. And people here have no imagination. They repeat whatever you say to them. Where I live I had a flower: She always spoke first...

Chapter XX

B ut it so happened that the little prince, having walked a long time through sand and rocks and snow, finally discovered a road. And all roads go to where there are people.

'Good morning,' he said.

It was a blossoming rose garden.

'Good morning,' said the roses.

The little prince gazed at them. All of them looked like his flower.

'Who are you?' he asked, astounded.

'We're roses,' the roses said.

'Ah!' said the little prince.

And he felt very unhappy. His flower had told him she was the only one of her kind in the whole universe. And here were five thousand of them, all just alike, in just one garden!

She would be very annoyed, he said to himself, if she saw this...She would cough terribly and pretend to be dying, to avoid being laughed at. And I'd have to pretend to be nursing her; otherwise, she'd really let herself die in order to humiliate me.

And then he said to himself, *I thought I was rich because I had just one flower, and all I own is an ordinary rose. That and my three volcanoes, which come up to my knee, one of which may be permanently extinct. It doesn't make me much of a prince...*And he lay down in the grass and wept.

Chapter XXI

It was then that the fox appeared.

'Good morning,' said the fox.

'Good morning,' the little prince answered politely, though when he turned around he saw nothing.

'I'm here,' the voice said, 'under the apple tree.'

'Who are you?' the little prince asked. 'You're very pretty...'

'I'm a fox,' the fox said.

'Come and play with me,' the little prince proposed. 'I'm feeling so sad.'

'I can't play with you,' the fox said. 'I'm not tamed.'

'Ah! Excuse me,' said the little prince. But upon reflection he added, 'What does tamed mean?"

'You're not from around here,' the fox said.

'What are you looking for?'

'I'm looking for people,' said the little prince. 'What does tamed mean?'

'People,' said the fox, 'have guns and they hunt. It's quite troublesome. And they also raise chickens. That's the only interesting thing about them. Are you looking for chickens?'

'No,' said the little prince, 'I'm looking for friends. What does *tamed* mean?'

'It's something that's been too often neglected. It means, "to create ties"...'

'"To create ties"?'

'That's right,' the fox said. 'For me you're only a little boy just like a hundred thousand other little boys. And I have no need of you. And you have no need of me, either. For you I'm only a fox like a hundred thousand other foxes. But if you tame me, we'll need each other. You'll be the only boy in the world for me. I'll be the only fox in the world for you...'

'I'm beginning to understand,' the little prince said. 'There's a flower...I think she's tamed me...'

'Possibly,' the fox said. 'On Earth, one sees all kinds of things.'

'Oh, this isn't on Earth,' the little prince said.

The fox seemed quite intrigued. 'On another planet?'

'Yes.'

'Are there hunters on that planet?'

'No.'

'Now that's interesting. And chickens?'

'No.'

'Nothing's perfect,' sighed the fox. But he returned to his idea. 'My life is monotonous. I hunt chickens; people hunt me. All chickens are just alike, and all men are just alike. So I'm rather bored. But if you tame me, my life will be filled with sunshine. I'll know the sound of footsteps that will be different from all the rest. Other footsteps send me back underground. Yours will call me out of my burrow like music. And then, look! You see the wheat fields over there? I don't eat bread. For me wheat is of no use whatever. Wheat fields say nothing to me. Which is sad[4]. But you have hair the colour of gold. So it will be wonderful, once you've tamed me! The wheat, which is golden, will remind me of you. And I'll love the sound of the wind in the wheat...'

The fox fell silent and stared at the little prince for a long while. 'Please...tame me!' he said.

'I'd like to,' the little prince replied, 'but I haven't much time. I have friends to find and so many things to learn.'

'The only things you learn are the things you tame,' said the fox. 'People haven't time to learn anything. They buy things ready-made in stores. But since there are no stores where you can buy friends, people no longer have friends. If you want a friend, tame me!'

'What do I have to do?' asked the little prince.

'You have to be very patient,' the fox answered. 'First

you'll sit down a little ways away from me, over there, in the grass. I'll watch you out of the corner of my eye, and you won't say anything. Language is the source of misunderstandings. But day by day, you'll be able to sit a little closer...'

The next day the little prince returned.

'It would have been better to return at the same time,' the fox said. 'For instance, if you come at four in the afternoon, I'll begin to be happy by three. The closer it gets to four, the happier I'll feel. By four I'll be all excited and worried; I'll discover what it costs to be happy! But if you come at any old time, I'll never know when I should prepare my heart...There must be rites.'

'What's a rite?' asked the little prince.

'That's another thing that's been too often neglected,' said the fox. 'It's the fact that one day is different from the other days, one hour from the other hours. My hunters, for example, have a rite. They dance with the village girls on Thursdays. So Thursday's a wonderful day: I can take a stroll all the way to the vineyards. If the hunters danced whenever they chose, the days would all be just alike, and I'd have no holiday at all.'

That was how the little prince tamed the fox. And when the time to leave was near:

'Ah!' the fox said. 'I shall weep.'

'It's your own fault,' the little prince said. 'I never wanted to do you any harm, but you insisted that I tame you...'

'Yes, of course,' the fox said.

'But you're going to weep!' said the little prince.

'Yes, of course,' the fox said.

'Then you get nothing out of it?'

'I get something,' the fox said, 'because of the colour of the wheat.' Then he added, 'Go look at the roses again. You'll understand that yours is the only rose in all the world. Then come back to say good-bye, and I'll make you the gift of a secret.'

The little prince went to look at the roses again.

'You're not at all like my rose. You're nothing at all yet,' he told them. 'No one has tamed you and you haven't tamed anyone. You're the way my fox was. He was just a fox like a hundred thousand others. But I've made him my friend, and now he's the only fox in all the world.'

And the roses were humbled.

'You're lovely, but you're empty,' he went on. 'One couldn't die for you. Of course, an ordinary passerby would think my rose looked just like you. But my rose, all on her own, is more important than all of you together, since she's the one I've watered. Since she's the one I put under glass.

Since she's the one I sheltered behind a screen. Since she's the one for whom I killed the caterpillars (except the two or three for butterflies). Since she's the one I listened to when she complained, or when she boasted, or even sometimes when she said nothing at all. Since she's *my* rose.'

And he went back to the fox.

'Good-bye,' he said.

'Good-bye,' said the fox. 'Here is my secret. It's quite simple: One sees clearly only with the heart. Anything essential is invisible to the eyes.'

'Anything essential is invisible to the eyes,' the little prince repeated, in order to remember.

'It's the time you spent on your rose that makes your rose so important.'

'It's the time I spent on my rose...,' the little prince repeated, in order to remember.

'People have forgotten this truth,' the fox said. 'But you mustn't forget it. You become responsible forever for what you've tamed. You're responsible for your rose...'

'I'm responsible for my rose...,' the little prince repeated, in order to remember.

Chapter XXII

'Good morning,' said the little prince.

'Good morning,' said the railway switchman.

'What is it that you do here?' asked the little prince.

'I sort the travellers into bundles of a thousand,' the switchman said. 'I dispatch the trains that carry them, sometimes to the right, sometimes to the left.'

And a brightly lit express train, roaring like thunder, shook the switchman's cabin.

'What a hurry they're in,' said the little prince. 'What are they looking for?'

'Not even the engineer on the locomotive knows,' the switchman said.

And another brightly lit express train thundered by in the opposite direction.

'Are they coming back already?' asked the little prince.

'It's not the same ones,' the switchman said. 'It's an exchange.'

'They weren't satisfied[5], where they were?' asked the little prince.

'No one is ever satisfied where he is,' the switchman said.

And a third brightly lit express train thundered past.

'Are they chasing the first travellers?' asked the little prince.

'They're not chasing anything,' the switchman said. They're sleeping in there, or else they're yawning. Only the children are pressing their noses against the windowpanes.'

'Only the children know what they're looking for,' said the little prince. 'They spend their time on a rag doll and it becomes very important, and if it's taken away from them, they cry...'

'They're lucky,' the switchman said.

Chapter XXIII

'Good morning,' said the little prince.
'Good morning,' said the salesclerk. This was a sales-clerk who sold pills invented to quench thirst. Swallow one a week and you no longer feel any need to drink.

'Why do you sell these pills?'

'They save so much time,' the salesclerk said. 'Experts have calculated that you can save fifty-three minutes a week.'

'And what do you do with those fifty-three minutes?'

'Whatever you like.'

'If I had fifty-three minutes to spend as I liked,' the little prince said to himself,
'I'd walk very slowly toward a water foun-tain...'

Chapter XXIV

It was now the eighth day since my crash landing in the desert, and I'd listened to the story about the salesclerk as I was drinking the last drop of my water supply.

'Ah,' I said to the little prince, 'your memories are very pleasant, but I haven't yet repaired my plane. I have nothing left to drink, and I, too, would be glad to walk very slowly toward a water fountain!'

'My friend the fox told me—'

'Little fellow, this has nothing to do with the fox!'

'Why?'

'Because we're going to die of thirst.'

The little prince didn't follow my reasoning, and answered me, 'It's good to have had a friend, even if you're going to die. Myself, I'm very glad to have had a fox for a friend.'

He doesn't realize the danger, I said to myself. *He's never hungry or thirsty. A little sunlight is enough for him...*

But the little prince looked at me and answered my thought. 'I'm thirsty, too... Let's find a well...'

I made an exasperated gesture. It is absurd looking for a well, at random, in the vastness of the desert. But even so, we started walking.

When we had walked for several hours in silence, night fell and stars began to appear. I noticed them as in a dream, being somewhat feverish on account of my thirst. The little prince's words danced in my memory.

'So you're thirsty, too?' I asked.

But he didn't answer my question. He merely said to me, 'Water can also be good for the heart...'

I didn't understand his answer, but I said nothing...I knew by this time that it was no use questioning him.

He was tired. He sat down. I sat down next to him. And after a silence, he spoke again. 'The stars are beautiful because of a flower you don't see...'

I answered, 'Yes, of course,' and without speaking another word I stared at the ridges of sand in the moonlight.

'The desert is beautiful,' the little prince added.

And it was true. I've always loved the desert. You sit

down on a sand dune. You see nothing. You hear nothing. And yet something shines, something sings in that silence. ...

'What makes the desert beautiful,' the little prince said, 'is that it hides a well somewhere...'

I was surprised by suddenly understanding that mysterious radiance of the sands. When I was a little boy I lived in an old house, and there was a legend that a treasure was buried in it somewhere. Of course, no one was ever able to find the treasure, perhaps no one even searched. But it cast a spell over that whole house. My house hid a secret in the depths of its heart. ...

'Yes,' I said to the little prince, 'whether it's a house or the stars or the desert, what makes them beautiful is invisible!'

'I'm glad,' he said, 'you agree with my fox.'

As the little prince was falling asleep, I picked him up in my arms, and started walking again. I was moved. It was as if I was carrying a fragile treasure. It actually seemed to me there was nothing more fragile on Earth. By the light of the moon, I gazed at that pale forehead, those closed eyes, those locks of hair trembling in the wind, and I said to myself, *What I'm looking at is only a shell. What's most important is invisible...*

As his lips parted in a half smile, I said to myself, again, *What moves me so deeply about this sleeping little prince is his loyalty to a flower—the image of a rose shining within him like the flame within a lamp, even when he's asleep...*And I realized he was even more fragile than I had thought. Lamps must be protected: A gust of wind can blow them out. ...

And walking on like that, I found the well at daybreak.

Chapter XXV

The little prince said, 'People start out in express trains, but they no longer know what they're looking for. Then they get all excited and rush around in circles...' And he added, 'It's not worth the trouble...'

The well we had come to was not at all like the wells of the Sahara. The wells of the Sahara are no more than holes dug in the sand. This one looked more like a village well. But there was no village here, and I thought I was dreaming.

'It's strange,' I said to the little prince, 'everything is ready: the pulley, the bucket, and the rope...'

He laughed, grasped the rope, and set the pulley working. And the pulley groaned the way an old

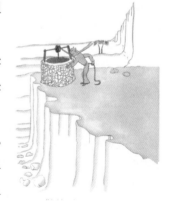

weather vane groans when the wind has been asleep a long time.

'Hear that?' said the little prince. 'We've awakened this well and it's singing.'

I didn't want him to tire himself out. 'Let me do that,' I said to him. 'It's too heavy for you.'

Slowly I hoisted the bucket to the edge of the well. I set it down with great care. The song of the pulley continued in my ears, and I saw the sun glisten on the still-trembling water.

'I'm thirsty for that water,' said the little prince. 'Let me drink some...'

And I understood what he'd been looking for!

I raised the bucket to his lips. He drank, eyes closed. It was as sweet as a feast. That water was more than merely a drink. It was born of our walk beneath the stars, of the song of the pulley, of the effort of my arms. It did the heart good, like a present. When I was a little boy, the Christmas-tree lights, the music of midnight mass, the tenderness of people's smiles made up, in the same way, the whole radiance of the Christmas present I received.

'People where you live,' the little prince said, 'grow five thousand roses in one garden...yet they don't find what they're looking for...'

'They don't find it,' I answered.

'And yet what they're looking for could be found in a single rose, or a little water...'

'Of course,' I answered.

And the little prince added, 'But eyes are blind. You have to look with the heart."

I had drunk the water. I could breathe easy now. The sand, at daybreak, is honey coloured. And that colour was making me happy, too. Why then did I also feel so sad?

'You must keep your promise,' said the little prince, sitting up again beside me.

'What promise?'

'You know...a muzzle for my sheep...I'm responsible for this flower!'

I took my drawings out of my pocket. The little prince glanced at them and laughed as he said, 'Your baobabs look more like cabbages.'

'Oh!' I had been so proud of the baobabs!

'Your fox...his ears...look more like horns...and they're too long!' And he laughed again.

'You're being unfair, my little prince,' I said. 'I never knew how to draw anything but boas from the inside and boas from the outside.'

'Oh, that'll be all right,' he said. 'Children understand.'

So then I drew a muzzle. And with a heavy heart I handed it to him. 'You've made plans I don't know about...'

But he didn't answer. He said, 'You know, my fall to Earth...Tomorrow will be the first anniversary...' Then, after a silence, he continued. 'I landed very near here...' And he blushed.

And once again, without understanding why, I felt a strange grief. However, a question occurred to me: 'Then it wasn't by accident that on the morning I met you, eight days ago, you were walking that way, all alone, a thousand miles from any inhabited region? Were you returning to the place where you fell to Earth?'

The little prince blushed again.

And I added, hesitantly, 'Perhaps on account...of the anniversary?'

The little prince blushed once more. He never answered questions, but when someone blushes, doesn't that mean 'yes'?

'Ah,' I said to the little prince, 'I'm afraid...'

But he answered, 'You must get to work now. You must get back to your engine. I'll wait here. Come back tomorrow night.'

But I wasn't reassured. I remembered the fox. You risk tears if you let yourself be tamed.

Chapter XXVI

Beside the well, there was a ruin, an old stone wall. When I came back from my work the next evening, I caught sight of my little prince from a distance. He was sitting on top of the wall, legs dangling. And I heard him talking. 'Don't you remember?' he was saying. 'This isn't exactly the place!' Another voice must have answered him then, for he replied, 'Oh yes, it's the right day, but this isn't the place...'

I continued walking toward the wall. I still could neither see nor hear anyone, yet the little prince answered again: 'Of course. You'll see where my tracks begin on the sand. Just wait for me there. I'll be there tonight.'

I was twenty yards from the wall and still saw no one.

Then the little prince said, after a silence, 'Your poison is good? You're sure it won't make me suffer long?'

I stopped short, my heart pounding, but I still didn't understand.

'Now go away,' the little prince said. 'I want to get down from here!'

Then I looked down toward the foot of the wall, and gave a great start! There, coiled in front of the little prince, was one of those yellow snakes that can kill you in thirty seconds. As I dug into my pocket for my revolver, I stepped back, but at the noise I made, the snake flowed over the sand like a trickling fountain, and without even hurrying, slipped away between the stones with a faint metallic sound.

I reached the wall just in time to catch my little prince in my arms, his face white as snow.

'What's going on here? You're talking to snakes now?'

I had loosened the yellow scarf he always wore. I had moistened his temples and made him drink some water. And now I didn't dare ask him anything more. He gazed at me with a serious expression and put his arms round my neck. I felt his heart beating like a dying bird's, when it's been shot. He said to me:

'I'm glad you found what was the matter with your engine. Now you'll be able to fly again. ...'

'How did you know?' I was just coming to tell him that I had been successful beyond all hope!

He didn't answer my question; all he said was 'I'm leaving today, too.' And then, sadly, 'It's much further...It's much more difficult.'

I realized that something extraordinary was happening. I was holding him in my arms like a little child, yet it seemed to me that he was dropping headlong into an abyss, and I could do nothing to hold him back.

His expression was very serious now, lost and remote. 'I have your sheep. And I have the crate for it. And the muzzle...' And he smiled sadly.

I waited a long time. I could feel that he was reviving a

little. 'Little fellow, you were frightened...' Of course he was frightened!

But he laughed a little. 'I'll be much more frightened tonight...'

Once again I felt chilled by the sense of something irreparable. And I realized I couldn't bear the thought of never hearing that laugh again. For me it was like a spring of fresh water in the desert.

'Little fellow, I want to hear you laugh again...'

But he said to me, 'Tonight, it'll be a year. My star will be just above the place where I fell last year...'

'Little fellow, it's a bad dream, isn't it? All this conversation with the snake and the meeting place and the star...'

But he didn't answer my question. All he said was 'The important thing is what can't be seen...'

'Of course...'

'It's the same as for the flower. If you love a flower that lives on a star, then it's good, at night, to look up at the sky. All the stars are blossoming.'

'Of course...'

'It's the same for the water. The water you gave me to drink was like music, on account of the pulley and the rope...You remember...It was good.'

'Of course...'

'At night, you'll look up at the stars. It's too small, where I live, for me to show you where my star is. It's better that way. My star will be...one of the stars, for you. So you'll like looking at all of them. They'll all be your friends. And besides, I have a present for you.' He laughed again.

'Ah, little fellow, little fellow, I love hearing that laugh!'

'That'll be my present. Just that...It'll be the same as for the water.'

'What do you mean?'

'People have stars, but they aren't the same. For travellers, the stars are guides. For other people, they're nothing but tiny lights. And for still others, for scholars, they're problems. For my businessman, they were gold. But all those stars are silent stars. You, though, you'll have stars like nobody else.'

'What do you mean?'

'When you look up at the sky at night, since I'll be living on one of them, since I'll be laughing on one of them, for you it'll be as if all the stars are laughing. You'll have stars that can laugh!'

And he laughed again.

'And when you're consoled (everyone eventually is consoled), you'll be glad you've known me. You'll always be my friend. You'll feel like laughing with me. And you'll open your window sometimes just for the fun of it...And your friends will be amazed to see you laughing while you're looking up at the sky. Then you'll tell them, "Yes, it's the stars; they always make me laugh!" And they'll think you're crazy. It'll be a nasty trick I played on you...'

And he laughed again.

'And it'll be as if I had given you, instead of stars, a lot of tiny bells that know how to laugh..."

And he laughed again. Then he grew serious once more. 'Tonight...you know...don't come.'

'I won't leave you.'

'It'll look as if I'm suffering. It'll look a little as if I'm dying. It'll look that way. Don't come to see that; it's not worth the trouble.'

'I won't leave you.'

But he was anxious. 'I'm telling you this...on account of the snake. He mustn't bite you. Snakes are nasty sometimes. They bite just for fun...'

'I won't leave you."

But something reassured him. 'It's true they don't have enough poison for a second bite...'

That night I didn't see him leave. He got away without making a sound. When I managed to catch up with him, he was walking fast, with determination. All he said was 'Ah, you're here.' And he took my hand. But he was still anxious. 'You were wrong to come. You'll suffer. I'll look as if I'm dead, and that won't be true...'

I said nothing.

'You understand. It's too far. I can't take this body with me. It's too heavy.'

I said nothing.

'But it'll be like an old abandoned shell. There's nothing sad about an old shell...'

I said nothing.

He was a little disheartened now. But he made one more effort.

'It'll be nice, you know. I'll be looking at the stars, too. All the stars will be wells with a rusty pulley. All the stars will pour out water for me to drink. ...'

I said nothing.

'And it'll be fun! You'll have five-hundred million little bells; I'll have five-hundred million springs of fresh water. ...'

And he, too, said nothing, because he was weeping. ...

'Here's the place. Let me go on alone.'

And he sat down because he was frightened. Then he said:

'You know...my flower...I'm responsible for her. And she's so weak! And so naive. She has four ridiculous thorns to defend her against the world...'

I sat down, too, because I was unable to stand any longer.

He said, 'There...That's all...'

He hesitated a little longer, then he stood up. He took a step. I couldn't move.

There was nothing but a yellow flash close to his ankle. He remained motionless for an instant. He didn't cry out. He fell gently, the way a tree falls. There wasn't even a sound, because of the sand.

Chapter XXVII

And now, of course, it's been six years already. ...I've never told this story before. The friends who saw me again were very glad to see me alive. I was sad, but I told them, 'It's fatigue.'

Now I'm somewhat consoled. That is...not entirely. But I know he did get back to his planet because at daybreak I didn't find his body. It wasn't such a heavy body. ...And at night I love listening to the stars. It's like five-hundred million little bells. ...

But something extraordinary has happened. When I drew that muzzle for the little prince, I forgot to put in the leather strap. He could never have fastened it on his sheep. And then I wonder, *What's happened there on his planet? Maybe the sheep has eaten the flower. ...*

Sometimes I tell myself, Of course not! *The little prince*

puts his flower under glass, and he keeps close watch over his sheep. ...Then I'm happy. And all the stars laugh sweetly.

Sometimes I tell myself, *Anyone might be distracted once in a while, and that's all it takes! One night he forgot to put her under glass, or else the sheep got out without making any noise, during the night.* ...Then the bells are all changed into tears!

It's all a great mystery. For you, who love the little prince, too. As for me, nothing in the universe can be the same if somewhere, no one knows where, a sheep we never saw has or has not eaten a rose. ...

Look up at the sky. Ask yourself, 'Has the sheep eaten the flower or not?' And you'll see how everything changes. ...

And no grown-up will ever understand how such a thing could be so important!

For me, this is the loveliest and the saddest landscape in the world. It's the same landscape as the one on the preceding page, but I've drawn it one more time in order to be sure you see it clearly. It's here that the little prince appeared on Earth, then disappeared.

Look at this landscape carefully to be sure of recognizing it, if you should travel to Africa someday, in the desert. And if you happen to pass by here, I beg you not to hurry past. Wait a little, just under the star! Then if a child comes to you, if he laughs, if he has golden hair, if he doesn't answer your questions, you'll know who he is. If this should happen, be kind! Don't let me go on being so sad: Send word immediately that he's come back. ...

THE END

Notes

1   kind
2   used formerly to address a king
3   red-checkered
4   That is sad.
5   Weren't they satisfied

小 王 子

Preface to the Chinese Translation
中文譯本序

《小王子》是法國作家聖埃克絮佩里（1900—1944）寫的一部童話。他寫了多部著名小説，同時也寫了這樣一部充滿智慧閃光的童話。

一個多世紀以前，安托萬・德・聖埃克絮佩里於 1900 年 6 月 29 日出生在法國里昂。他在姨媽家度過了童年時代，又去瑞士讀中學。回國後，一邊在巴黎美術學院就學，一邊準備報考海軍學院。結果沒有通過口試，未能如願進入海軍學院。他沒能當成海軍，卻成了一名空軍。因為他 1921 年應徵服義務兵役，到斯特拉斯堡附近的空軍基地，擔任過空軍地勤人員和飛行員。

他 1923 年退役後，先後從事多種不同的職業。1925 年開始寫作，第一部作品就是以飛行為題材的。

1926 年，聖埃克絮佩里進入拉泰科埃爾航空公司，擔任法國圖盧茲至塞內加爾達喀爾航空郵班的飛行員，繼而被派往摩洛哥擔任航線中途站站長。在此期間，出版小說《南方郵件》（1929）。後來他隨同梅爾莫茲、吉約姆等老資格的飛行員前往南美洲開闢新航線。1931年出版小說《夜航》，從此他在文學上的名聲就大起來了。

1935年，拉泰科埃爾公司倒閉。聖埃克絮佩里隨公司人員並入新成立的法國航空公司後，曾嘗試打破巴黎至西貢的飛行時間記錄，沒有成功。1938年在重建紐約至火地島航線途中身受重傷，於紐約治療多月後才開始康復。出版《人類的大地》（1939）。

第二次世界大戰期間他加入法國空軍。得悉貝當政府簽訂屈辱的停戰協定後，輾轉去紐約開始流亡生活。在這期間，他寫出了《空軍飛行員》、《給一個人質的信》、《小王子》（1943）等作品。1944年重返同盟國地中海空軍部隊，因明顯超齡，沒有被列入飛行員編制。但他堅決要求駕機上天，經司令部特許終於如願。就在1944年的7月31日，他從科西嘉島的博爾戈出發，隻身前往里昂地區執行偵察任務。飛機駛上湛藍的天空，就此再也沒有回來。

《小王子》是一部兒童文學作品，也是一部寫給成年人看的童話，用聖埃克絮佩里自己的話來說，是寫給“還是孩子時”的那個大人看的文學作品。整部小說充滿詩意的憂鬱、淡淡的哀愁，用明白如話的語言寫出了引人深思的哲理和令人感動的韻味。這種韻味，具體說來，就是簡單的形式和深刻的內涵的相契合。整部童話，文字很乾淨，甚至純淨，形式很簡潔，甚至簡單。因此，這部童話的譯文，也應該是明白如話的。

不過要做到這一點，並不容易。舉個例子來說，第二十一章裏狐狸提出了一個很重要的（後來反覆出現的）概念，法文中用的是 apprivoiser，這個詞當然可以譯成"馴養"或"馴服"。這樣譯，有詞典為依據。然而問題在於，作者到底是在怎樣的語境中使用這個詞的呢？要弄明白這個問題，勢必就得細細品味上下文，把這個詞放在上下文中間去體會它的含義。而這時候，譯者很容易"當局者迷"。我一開始就迷惘過 —— 先是譯作"馴養"，然後換成"養服"。放在上下文中間，自己也覺得是有些突兀，但轉念一想，既然是個哲學概念（狐狸在這一章中以智者的形象出現），有些突兀恐怕也可以容忍吧。後來有朋友看了初稿，對這個詞提出意見，還跟我仔細地討論這段文字的內涵，我受他的啟發，才決定改用"跟……處熟"的譯法。這個譯法未必理想，但我們最終還是沒能找到更滿意的譯法。暫且，就是它吧。

所有的大人起先都是孩子 —— 但願我們都能記得這一點。

周克希

獻給萊翁‧維爾特

　　請孩子們原諒我把這本書獻給了一個大人。我有一個很認真的理由：這個大人是我在世界上最好的朋友。我還有另外一個理由：這個大人甚麼都懂，即使是給孩子看的書他也懂。我的第三個理由是：這個大人生活在法國，正在捱餓受凍。他很需要得到安慰。倘若所有這些理由加在一起還不夠，那我願意把這本書獻給還是孩子時的這個大人。所有的大人起先都是孩子（可是他們中間不大有人記得這一點）。因此我把題獻改為：

　　獻給還是小男孩的　萊翁‧維爾特

第一章

我六歲那年，在一本描寫原始森林的名叫《真實的故事》的書上，看見過一幅精彩的插圖，畫的是一條蟒蛇在吞吃一頭猛獸。我現在把牠照樣畫在上面。

書中寫道："蟒蛇把獵物囫圇吞下，嚼都不嚼。然後牠就無法動彈，躺上六個月來消化牠們。"

當時，我對叢林裏的奇妙景象想得很多，於是我也用彩色鉛筆畫了我的第一幅畫：我的作品 1 號。它就像這樣：

我把這幅傑作給大人看，問他們我的圖畫嚇不嚇人。

他們回答説："一頂帽子怎麼會嚇人呢？"

我畫的不是一頂帽子。我畫的是一條蟒蛇在消化大象。於是我把蟒蛇肚子的內部畫出來，好讓這些大人看得明白。他們老是要人給他們解釋。我的作品 2 號是這樣的：

那些大人勸我別再畫蟒蛇，別管牠是剖開的，還是沒剖開的，全都丟開。他們説，我還是把心思放在地理、歷史、算術和語法上好。就這樣，我才六歲，就放棄了輝煌的畫家生涯。作品1號和作品2號都沒成功，我洩了氣。那些大人自己甚麼也弄不懂，老要孩子們一遍一遍給他們解釋，真煩人。

我只好另外選擇一個職業，學會了開飛機。世界各地我差不多都飛過。的確，地理學對我非常有用。我一眼就能認出哪是中國，哪是亞利桑那。要是夜裏迷了路，這很有用。

就這樣，我這一生中，跟好多嚴肅的人打過很多交道。我在那些大人中間生活過很長時間。我仔細地觀察過他們。觀察下來印象並沒好多少。

要是碰上一個人，看上去頭腦稍為清楚些，我就拿出一直保存着的作品1號，讓他試試看。我想知道，他是不是真的能看懂。可是人家總是回答我：“這是一頂帽子。”這時候，我就不跟他說甚麼蟒蛇啊，原始森林啊，星星啊，都不說了。我就說些他懂的事情。我跟他說橋、高爾夫、政治，還有領帶。於是大人覺得很高興，認識了這麼個通情達理的人。

第二章

我孤獨地生活着，沒有一個真正談得來的人，直到六年前，有一次飛機出了故障，降落在撒哈拉大沙漠。發動機裏有樣甚麼東西碎掉了。因為我身邊既沒有機械師，也沒有乘客，我就打算單人匹馬來完成一項困難的修復工作。這在我是個生死攸關的問題。我帶的水只夠喝一星期了。

第一天晚上，我睡在這片遠離人煙的大沙漠上，比靠一塊船板在大海中漂流的遇難者還孤獨。所以，當天曚曚亮，有個奇怪的聲音輕輕把我喚醒的時候，你們可以想像我有多麼驚訝。這個聲音說：

"對不起……請給我畫隻綿羊！"

"嗯！"

"請給我畫隻綿羊……"

我像遭了雷擊似的，猛地一下子跳了起來。我用力揉了揉眼睛，仔細地看了看。只見一個從沒見過的小人兒，正一本正經地看着我呢。後來我給他畫了一幅非常出色的肖像，就是旁邊的這幅。不過我的畫，當然遠遠不及本人可愛。這不是我的錯。我的畫家生涯在六歲那年就讓大人給斷送了，除了畫剖開和不剖開的蟒蛇，後來再沒畫過甚麼。

我吃驚地瞪大眼睛看着他。你們別忘記，這裏離有人住的地方很遠很遠呢。可是這個小人兒，看上去並不像迷了路，也不像累得要命、餓得要命、渴得要命或怕得要命。他一點不像在遠離人類居住地的沙漠裏迷路的孩子。等我總算說得出話時，我對他說：

"可是……你在這裏做甚麼呢？"

他輕聲輕氣地又說了一遍，好像那是件很要緊的事情：

"對不起……請給我畫一隻綿羊……"

受到神秘事物強烈衝擊時，一個人是不敢不聽從的。儘管在我看來，離一切有人住的地方遠而又遠，又處於死亡的威脅之下，在這裏想到畫畫真是匪夷所思，可是我還是從口袋裏掏出一張紙、一支鋼筆。但我想起我只學了地理、歷史、算術和語法，所以我就（有點沒好氣地）對那小人兒說，我不會畫畫。他回答說：

"沒關係。請給我畫一隻綿羊。"

我因為從沒畫過綿羊，就在我只會畫的兩張圖畫裏挑一張給他畫了：沒剖開的蟒蛇圖。但我聽到小人兒下面說的話，簡直驚呆了：

"不對！不對！我不要在蟒蛇肚子裏的大象。蟒蛇很危險，大象呢，太佔地方。在我那裏，甚麼都是小小的。我要的是一隻綿羊。請給我畫一隻綿羊。"

我只得畫了起來。他專心地看了一會，然後説：

"不對！這隻羊已經病得不輕了。另外畫一隻吧。"

我畫了右面的這隻。

我的朋友溫和地笑了，口氣寬容地説：

"你看看⋯⋯這隻不是綿羊，是山羊。頭上長着角⋯⋯"

於是我又畫了一張。

但這一張也跟前幾張一樣，沒能通過：

"這隻太老了。我要一隻可以活得很久的綿羊。"

我已經沒有耐心了，因為我急於要去把發動機拆下來，所以我就胡亂畫了一張。

我隨口説道：

"這個呢，是個箱子。你要的綿羊就在裏面。"

但是令我吃驚的是，這個小評判的臉上頓時變得容光煥發了：

"我要的就是這個！你説，這隻綿羊會要很多草嗎？"

"問這做甚麼？"

"因為我那裏樣樣都很小⋯⋯"

"肯定夠了。我給你的是隻很小的綿羊。"

他低下頭去看那幅畫：

"不算太小……看！牠睡着了……"

就這樣，我認識了小王子。

第三章

很久以後，我才弄明白他是從哪裏來的。

這個小王子，對我提了好多問題，而對我的問題總像沒聽見似的。我是從他偶然漏出來的那些話裏，一點一點知道這一切的。比如，他第一次看見我的飛機時（我沒畫我的飛機，對我來説，這樣的畫實在太複雜了），就問我：

"這是甚麼東西？"

"這不是甚麼東西，它會飛。這是一架飛機，是我的飛機。"

我自豪地講給他聽，我在天上飛。他聽了就大聲説：

"怎麼！你是天上掉下來的？"

"是的，"我謙虛地説。

"喔！真有趣……"

小王子發出一陣清脆的笑聲，這可把我惹惱了。我不喜歡別人拿我的不幸逗趣。接着他又説：

"這麼説，你也是從天上來的！你從哪個星球來？"

我腦子裏閃過一個念頭，他的降臨之謎好像有了線索，我突如其來地發問：

"那你是從別的星球來的？"

可是他沒有回答。他看着我的飛機，輕輕地點了點頭：

"是啊，就靠它，你來的地方不會太遠……"

説着，他出神地遐想了很久。然後，從袋裏拿出我畫的綿羊，全神貫注地凝望着這寶貝。

你想想看，這個跟"別的星球"有關，説了一半又欲言又止的話，會讓我多麼驚訝啊。我竭力想多知道一些：

"你從哪裏來，我的小傢伙？'我那裏'是哪裏？你要把我畫的綿羊帶到哪裏去？"

他若有所思地沉默了一會，然後開口對我説：

"你給了我這個箱子，這就好了，晚上可以給牠當屋子。"

"當然。要是你乖，我還會給你一根繩子，白天可以把牠拴住。木椿也有。"

這個提議好像使小王子很不以為然：

"拴住？真是怪念頭！"

"但要是你不把牠拴住，牠就會到處跑，還會跑丟了……"

我的朋友又格格地笑了起來：

“你叫牠往哪裏跑呀？”

“到處跑。筆直往前……”

這時，小王子一本正經地說：

“那也沒關係，我那裏就一丁點大！”

然後，他又說了一句，語氣中彷彿有點憂鬱：

“就是筆直往前跑，也跑不了多遠……”

第四章

我由此知道了另一件很重要的事情：他居住的星球比一座房子大不了多少！

這並沒讓我感到很吃驚。我知道，除了像地球、木星、火星、金星這些取了名字的大星球，還有成千上萬的星球，它們有時候非常非常小，用望遠鏡都不大看得見。天文學家找到其中的一個星球，給它編一個號碼就算名字了。比如說，他把它叫作"3251號小行星"。

我有很可靠的理由，足以相信小王子原先住的那個星球，就是B612號小行星。這顆小行星只在1909年被人用望遠鏡望見過一次，那人是一個土耳其天文學家。

當時，他在一次國際天文學大會上作了長篇論證。可是就為了他的服裝的緣故，誰也不信他的話。大人哪，就是這樣。

幸好，有一個土耳其獨裁者下令，全國百姓都要穿歐洲的服裝，違令者處死，這一下B612號小行星的名聲總算保全了。那個天文學家在 1920 年重新做了報告，穿着一套非常體面的西裝。這一次所有的人都同意了他的觀點。

我之所以要跟你們一五一十地介紹 B612 號小行星，還把它的編號也講得明明白白，完全是為了大人。那些大人就喜歡數字。你跟他們講起一個新朋友，他們總愛問些無關重要的問題。他們不會問你："他說話的聲音是怎樣的？他喜歡玩哪些遊戲？他是不是收集蝴蝶標本？"他們問的是："他幾歲？有幾個兄弟？他有多重？他父親賺多少錢？"這樣問過以後，他們就以為了解他了。你要是對大人說："我看見一幢漂亮的房子，紅磚牆，窗前種着天竺葵，屋頂上停着鴿子……"他們想像不出這幢房子是怎樣的。你必須這麼跟他們說："我看見一幢十萬法郎的房子。"他們馬上會大聲嚷嚷："多漂亮的房子！"

所以，如果你對他們說："小王子是存在的，證據就是他那麼可愛，他格格地笑，他還想要一隻綿羊。一個人想要有隻綿羊，這就是他存在的證據嘛，"他們會聳聳肩膀，只當你還是個孩子！可是你若對他們說："他來自 B612 號小行星，"他們就會深信不疑，不再問這問那地煩你了。他們就是這樣。不必怪他們。孩子應該對大人多多原諒才是。

不過，當然，我們懂得生活，我們才不把數字放在眼裏呢！我真願意像講童話那樣來開始講這個故事。我真想這樣說：

"從前呀，有一個小王子，住在一個跟他身體差不多大的星球上，他想有個朋友……"對那些懂得生活的人來說，這樣聽上去會真實得多。

　　我不想人家輕率地來讀我這本書。我講述這段往事時，心情是很難過的。我的朋友帶着他的綿羊已經離去六年了。我之所以在這裏細細地描述他，就是為了不要忘記他。忘記朋友是件令人傷心的事情。並不是人人都有過一個朋友的。再說，我早晚也會變得像那些只關心數字的大人一樣的。也正是為了這個緣故，我買了一盒顏料和一些鉛筆。到了我這年紀再重握畫筆，是很吃力的，況且當初我只畫過剖開和沒剖開的蟒蛇，還是六歲那年！當然，我一定要盡力把它們畫得像一些。但做不做得到，我可說不定。有時這一張還行，那一張就不大像了。比如說，身材我就有點記不準確了。這一張裏小王子畫得太高了。那一張呢太矮了。衣服的顏色也很讓我發生困難。我只好信手拿起色筆這裏試一下，那裏試一下。到頭來，有些最要緊的細部，說不定都弄錯了。不過這一切，大家都要原諒我才是。我的朋友從來不跟我解釋甚麼。他大概以為我是跟他一樣的。可是，很遺憾，我已經看不見箱子裏面的綿羊了。我也許已經有點像那些大人了。我一定是老了。

第五章

每天我都會知道一些情況，或者是關於他的星球，或者是關於他怎麼離開那裏、怎麼來到這裏。這些情況，都是一點一點，碰巧知道的。比如說，在第三天，我知道了猴麵包樹的悲劇。

這一次，起因又是那隻綿羊，因為小王子突然向我發問，好像憂心忡忡似的：

"綿羊當真吃灌木嗎？"

"對。當真。"

"啊！我真高興。"

我不明白，綿羊吃灌木，為甚麼會這麼重要。小王子接着又說：

"這麼說，牠們也吃猴麵包樹啦？"

我告訴小王子，猴麵包樹不是灌木，而是像教堂那麼高的大樹，他就是領一群大象來，也吃不完一棵猴麵包樹呢。

領一群大象來的想法，惹得小王子笑了起來：

"那必須讓牠們疊羅漢了……"

不過他很聰明，接着又説：

"猴麵包樹在長高以前，起初也是小小的。"

"一點不錯。可是你為甚麼想讓綿羊去吃小猴麵包樹呢？"

他回答説："咦！這還不明白嗎！"就像這是件不言而喻的事情。可是我自己要弄懂這個問題，還着實須動一番腦筋呢。

原來，在小王子的星球上，就像在別的星球上一樣，有好的植物，也有不好的植物。結果呢，好植物有好種子，壞植物有壞種子。而種子是看不見的。它們悄悄地睡在地底下，直到有一天，其中有一顆忽然想起要醒了……於是它舒展身子，最先羞答答地朝太陽伸出一枝天真可愛的嫩苗。假如那是蘿蔔或玫瑰的幼苗，可以讓它愛怎麼生長就怎麼生長。不過，假如那是一株不好的植物，一認出就必須拔掉它。在小王子的星球上有一種可怕的種子……就是猴麵包樹的種子。星球的土壤裏有好多猴麵包樹種子。而猴麵包樹長得很快，動手稍稍一慢，就別想再除掉它了。它會佔滿整個星球，根枝鑽來鑽去，四處蔓延。要是這顆星球太小，而猴麵包樹又太多，它們就會把星球撐裂。

"這就必須有個嚴格的約束了，"小王子後來告訴我説。

"你早晨梳洗好以後，就該仔仔細細地給星球梳洗了。猴麵包樹小的時候，跟玫瑰幼苗是很像的，那你就必須給自己立個規矩，只要分清了哪是玫瑰，哪是猴麵包樹，就馬上把猴麵包樹拔掉。這個工作很單調，但並不難。"

有一天，他勸我好好畫一幅畫，好讓我那裏的孩子們都知道這回事。"要是他們有一天出門旅行，"他對我説，"説不定會用得着。有時候，你把一件該做的事耽擱一下，也沒甚麼關係。可是，碰到猴麵包樹，這就要造成一場災難了。我知道有一個星球，上面住着一個懶人。有三株幼苗他沒在意……"

在小王子的指點下，我畫好了那顆星球。我一向不願意擺出説教的姿態。可是對猴麵包樹的危害，一般人都不了解，要是有人碰巧迷了路停在一顆小行星上，情況就會變得極其嚴峻。所以這一次，我破例拋開了矜持。我説："孩子們！小心猴麵包樹啊！"這幅畫我畫得格外賣力，就是為了提醒朋友們有這麼一種危險存在，他們也像我一樣，對在身邊潛伏了很久的危險一直毫不察覺。要讓大家明白這道理，我多花點時間也是值得的。你們也許會想："在這本書裏，別的畫為甚麼都不及這幅奔放有力呢？"回答很簡單：我同樣努力了，但沒能成功。畫猴麵包樹時，我內心非常焦急，情緒就受到了感染。

第六章

哦，小王子！就這樣，我一點一點知道了你那段憂鬱的生活。過去很長的時間裏，你惟一的樂趣就是觀賞夕陽沉落的溫柔晚景。這個新的細節，我是在第四天早晨知道的。當時你對我説：

"我喜歡看日落。我們去看一次日落吧……"

"可是必須等……"

"等甚麼？"

"等太陽下山呀。"

開始，你顯得很驚奇，隨後你自己笑了起來。你對我説：

"我還以為在家鄉呢！"

可不是。大家都知道，美國的中午，在法國正是黃昏。要是能在一分鐘內趕到法國，就可以看到日落。可惜法國實在太遠了。而在你那小小的星球上，你只要把椅子挪動幾步就行了。那樣，你就隨時可以看到你想看的夕陽餘暉……

“有一天，我看了四十三次日落！”

過了一會，你又說：

“你知道……一個人感到非常憂傷的時候，他就喜歡看日落……”

“這麼說，看四十三次的那天，你感到非常憂傷？”

但是小王子沒有回答。

第七章

第五天，還是羊的事情，把小王子生活的秘密向我揭開了。他好像有個問題默默地思索了很久，終於得出了結論，突然無緣無故問我：

"綿羊既然吃灌木，那牠也吃花兒？"

"牠碰到甚麼吃甚麼。"

"連有刺的花兒也吃？"

"對。有刺的也吃。"

"那麼，刺有甚麼用呢？"

我不知道該怎麼回答。當時我正忙着要從發動機上卸下一顆擰得太緊的螺絲釘。我發現故障似乎很嚴重，飲用水也快完了。我擔心會發生最壞的情況，心裏很着急。

"那麼，刺有甚麼用呢？"

小王子只要提了一個問題，就從不放棄，一定要得到答案。而那個螺絲釘正弄得我很惱火，我就隨口回答了一句：

"刺呀，甚麼用都沒有，純粹是花兒想出壞主意啦。"

"喔！"

但他沉默了一會以後，忿然衝着我説：

"我不信你的話！花兒是纖弱的，天真的。它們想盡量保護自己。它們以為有了刺就會顯得很厲害……"

我沒作聲。我當時想："要是這顆螺絲釘再不鬆開，我就一鎚子敲掉它。"小王子又打斷了我的思路：

"但是你，你卻認為花兒……"

"行了！行了！我甚麼也不認為！我只是隨口説説。我正忙着做正事呢！"

他驚愕地望着我。

"正事！"

他看我握着鎚子，手指沾滿油污，俯身對着一個他覺得非常醜陋的物件。

"你説話就像那些大人！"

這話使我有些難堪。而他毫不留情地接着説：

"你甚麼都分不清……你把甚麼都攪在一起！"

他真的氣極了，一頭金髮在風中搖曳：

"我到過一個星球，上面住着一個紅臉先生。他從沒聞過花香。他從沒望過星星。他從沒愛過一個人。除了算賬，他甚麼事也沒做過。他整天像你一樣説個沒完沒了：'我有正事要做！我有正事要做！'變得驕氣十足。但是這算不上是一個人，他是個蘑菇。"

"是個甚麼？"

"是個蘑菇！"

小王子這一會氣得臉色發白了。

"幾百萬年以前，花兒就長刺了。可是幾百萬年以前，羊也早就在吃花兒了。刺甚麼用也沒有，那花兒為甚麼要花那麼大的力氣去長刺呢，把這弄明白難道不是正事嗎？綿羊和花兒的戰爭難道不重要嗎？這難道不比那個胖子紅臉先生的計算更重要，更是正事嗎？還有，如果我認識一朵世上獨一無二的花兒，除了我的星球，哪裏都找不到這樣的花兒，而有天早上，一隻小羊甚至都不明白自己在做甚麼，就一口把花兒吃掉了，這難道不重要嗎！"

他的臉紅了起來，接着往下說：

"如果有一個人愛上一朵花兒，好幾百萬好幾百萬顆星星中間，只有一顆上面長着這朵花兒，那他只要望着許許多多星星，就會感到很幸福。他對自己說：'我的花兒就在其中的一顆星星上……'可是若綿羊吃掉了這朵花兒，這對他來說，就好像滿天的星星突然一下子都熄滅了！這難道不重要嗎！"

他說不下去了，突然抽抽咽咽地哭了起來。夜色降臨。我放下手中的工具。鎚子呀，螺絲釘呀，口渴呀，死亡呀，我全都丟在了腦後。在一顆星星，在一顆我所在的行星，在這個地球上，有一個小王子需要安慰！我把他抱在懷裏。我搖着他，對他説："你愛的那朵花兒不會有危險的……我會給你的綿羊畫一隻嘴罩……我會給你的花兒畫一個護欄……我……"我不知道再説甚麼好了。我覺得自己笨嘴笨舌的。我不知道怎樣去接近他，打動他……淚水的世界，是多麼神秘啊。

第八章

我很快就對這朵花兒有了更多了解。在小王子的星球上，過去一直長着些很簡單的花兒，這些花兒只有一層花瓣，不佔地方，也不妨礙任何人。某個早晨她們會在草叢中綻放，一到晚上又都悄悄凋謝了。有一天，一顆不知從哪裏來的種子發了芽，長出的嫩苗跟別的幼苗都不一樣。小王子小心翼翼觀察着這株嫩苗，它說不定是猴麵包樹的一枝幼芽呢。但是這株嫩苗很快就不再長大，漸漸含苞待放。小王子眼看着它綻出一個很大很大的花蕾，心想這花蕾裏一定會出現奇妙的景象，可是這朵花兒留在綠色的花萼裏面，拖拖拉拉地打扮個沒完。她精心挑選着自己的顏色，慢吞吞地穿上衣裙，一片一片地理順花瓣。她不願像虞美人，即一種夏天開花的植物那樣，一亮相就是滿臉皺紋。她要讓自己美艷照人地來到世間。噢！對。她很愛美！她那神秘的裝扮，就這樣日復一日地延續着。然後，有一天早晨，太陽剛升起的時候，她綻放了。

她悉心打扮了那麼久，這一會卻打着哈欠説：

"啊！我剛睡醒……真對不起……頭髮還是亂蓬蓬的
……"

這時，小王子的愛慕之情油然而生：

"您真美！"

"可不是嗎，"花兒柔聲答道，"我是跟太陽同時出生的
嘛……"

小王子感覺到了她不太謙虛，不過她實在太楚楚動人
了！

"我想，現在該是用早餐的時間了，"她隨即又説，"麻
煩您也給我……"

小王子很不好意思，於是就打來一壺清水，給這朵花兒
澆水。

就這樣，她帶着點多疑的虛榮心，很快就把他折磨得很
苦惱。比如説，有一天説起她的四根刺，她對小王子説：

"那些老虎，讓牠們張着爪子來好了！"

"我的星球上沒有老虎，"小王子頂了她一句，"再説，
老虎也不吃草呀。"

"我不是草，"花兒柔聲答道。

"對不起……"

"我不怕老虎，可是我怕風。您沒有風障嗎？"

"怕風……一棵植物像這個樣，那可慘了，"小王子輕聲說，"花兒可真難伺候……"

"晚上您要把我罩起來。您這裏很冷。又沒安頓好。我來的那地方……"

可是她沒說下去。她來的時候是顆種子。她不可能知道別的世界是怎麼樣的。讓人發現她說的謊這麼不高明，她又羞又惱，就咳了兩三聲嗽，想讓小王子覺得理虧：

"風障呢？"

"我正要去拿，可是您跟我說上話了！"

於是她咳得更重了些，不管怎麼說，她非讓他感到內疚不可。

就這樣，小王子儘管真心真意喜歡這朵花兒，可還是很快就對她起了疑心。他對那些無關重要的話太當真了，結果自己很苦惱。

"我本來不該去聽她說甚麼的，"有一天他對我說了心裏話，"花兒說的話，是不應該信的。花兒是讓人看，讓人聞的。這朵花兒讓我的星球芳香四溢，我卻不會享受這快樂。老虎爪子那些話，惹得我那麼生氣，其實我該同情她才是……"

他還對我說：

"我當時甚麼也不懂！看她這個人，應該看她做甚麼，而不是聽她說甚麼。她給了我芳香，給了我光彩。我真不該逃走！我本該猜到她那小小花招背後的一片柔情。花兒總是這麼表裏不一！可惜當時我太年輕，還不懂得怎麼去愛她。"

第九章

我想他是趁一群野鳥遷徙的機會出走的。出發的那天早晨，他把星球收拾得井井有條。他仔細地疏通了活火山。星球上有兩座活火山，熱早餐很方便。還有一座死火山。不過，正像他所説的："誰都很難説！"所以這座死火山也照樣要疏通。火山疏通過了，就會緩緩地、均勻地燃燒，不會噴發。火山噴發跟煙囪冒火是一樣的。當然，在地球上，我們實在太小了，沒法去疏通火山。它們造成那麼多麻煩，就是由於這個緣故。

小王子還拔掉了剛長出來的幾株猴麵包樹幼苗。他心情有點憂鬱，心想這一走就再也回不來了。所有這些習慣的工作，這天早上都顯得格外親切。而當他最後一次給花兒澆水，準備給它蓋上罩子的時候，他只覺得想哭。

"再見啦，"他對花兒説。

可是她沒有回答。

"再見啦，"他又説了一遍。

花兒咳嗽起來。但不是由於感冒。

"我以前太傻了，"她終於開口了，"請你原諒我。但願你能幸福。"

他感到吃驚的是，居然沒有一聲責備。他舉着罩子，茫然不知所措地站在那裏。他不懂這般恬淡的柔情。

"是的，我愛你，"花兒對他説，"但由於我的過錯，你一點也沒領會。這沒甚麼要緊。不過你也和我一樣傻。但願你能幸福……把這罩子放在一邊吧，我用不着它了。"

"可是風……"

"我並不是那麼容易感冒的……夜晚的新鮮空氣對我有好處。我是一朵花兒。"

"可是那些蟲子和野獸……"

"我既然想認識蝴蝶，就應該受得了兩三條毛蟲。我覺得這樣挺好。要不然有誰來看我呢？你，你到時候已經走得遠遠的了。至於野獸，我根本不怕。我也有爪子。"

説着，她天真地讓他看那四根刺。隨後她又説：

"別拖拖拉拉的，讓人心煩。你已經決定要走了。那就走吧。"

因為她不願意讓他看見自己流淚。她是一朵如此驕傲的花兒……

第十章

這顆星球附近，還有 325 號、326 號、327 號、328 號、329 號和 330 號小行星。於是他開始拜訪這些星球，好給自己找點事做，也好增長些見識。

第一顆小行星上住着一個國王。這個國王身穿紫紅鑲邊白鼬皮長袍，端坐在一張簡樸而又氣派莊嚴的王座上。

"哈！來了一個臣民，"國王看見小王子，大聲叫了起來。

可是小王子覺得納悶：

"他以前從沒見過我，怎麼會認識我呢？"

他不知道，對國王來說，世界是非常簡單的。所有的人都是臣民。

"你走近點，讓我好好看看你，"國王説，他覺得非常驕傲，因為他終於成了某個人的國王。

小王子朝四下裏看看，想找個地方坐下來，可是整個星球都被那襲華麗的白鼬皮長袍佔滿了。所以他只好站着，不過，由於他累了，就打了個哈欠。

"在國王面前打哈欠，有違宮廷禮儀，"國王對他說，"我禁止你打哈欠。"

"我沒忍住，"小王子歉疚地說，"我走了好長的路，一直沒睡覺……"

"那麼，"國王對他說，"我命令你打哈欠。我有好幾年沒見人打哈欠了。我覺得打哈欠挺好玩。來！再打個哈欠。這是命令。"

"我給嚇着了……打不出……"小王子漲紅着臉說。

"嗯！嗯！"國王回答說。"那麼我……我命令你這一會打哈欠，這一會……"

他低聲自言自語，看上去不大高興。

國王其實是要別人尊重他的權威。他不能容忍別人不服從命令。他是個專制的君主。不過，因為他很善良，他下的命令都是通情達理的。

"要是我命令，"這番話他說得流暢極了，"要是我命令一個將軍變成一隻海鳥，那個將軍不服從，這就不是那個將軍的錯，這是我的錯。"

"我可以坐下嗎？"小王子怯生生地問。

"我命令你坐下，"國王回答他說，莊重地挪了挪白鼬皮長袍的下襬。

可是小王子感到很奇怪。這麼小的星球，國王能統治甚麼呢?

"陛下……"他説,"請允許我向您提個……"

"我命令你向我提問題,"國王趕緊搶着説。

"陛下……您統治甚麼呢?"

"一切,"國王的回答簡單明瞭。

"一切?"

國王小心翼翼地做了個手勢,指了指他的行星、其他的行星和所有的星星。

"全歸您統治?"小王子問。

"全歸我統治……"國王回答説。

因為他不僅是一國的專制君主,還是宇宙的君主。

"那些星星都服從您?"

"當然,"國王回答説,"我一下命令,它們馬上就服從。我不能容忍紀律渙散。"

這樣的權力使小王子驚歎不已。他如果擁有這樣的權力,那麼一天就不是看四十三次,而是七十二次,一百次,甚至兩百次日落,連椅子都不用挪一挪!由於想起被他遺棄的小星球,他有點難過,所以就壯着膽子向國王提出一個請求:

"我想看一次日落……請您為我……命令太陽下山……"

"要是我命令一個將軍像蝴蝶一樣從一朵花兒飛到另一朵花兒,或者讓他寫一部悲劇,或者讓他變成一隻海鳥,而這個將軍拒不執行命令，那是誰，是他還是我的錯呢？"

"那是您的錯，"小王子肯定地説。

"正是如此。必須讓每個人去做他能做到的事情，"國王接着説。"權威首先必須建立在合理的基礎上。如果你命令你的老百姓都去投海，他們就會造反。我之所以有權讓人服從，就是因為我的命令都是合情合理的。"

"那麼我想看的日落呢？"小王子想起了這件事，他對自己提過的問題是不會忘記的。

"你會看到日落的。我會要它下山的。不過按照我的統治原則，要等到條件成熟的時候。"

"要等到甚麼時候呢？"小王子問。

"嗯！嗯！"國王先翻看一本厚厚的曆書，然後回答説，"嗯！嗯！要等到，大概……大概……要等到今晚大概七點四十分！你會看到它乖乖地服從我的命令的。"

小王子打了個哈欠。看不到日落，讓他感到挺遺憾。再説他也已經有點膩煩了：

"我在這裏沒甚麼事好做了，"他對國王説。"我要走了！"

"別走，"國王回答説，他有了一個臣民，正驕傲着呢。"別走，我任命你當大臣！"

"甚麼大臣？"

"這個……司法大臣！"

"可是這裏沒有人要審判呀！"

"那可説不定，"國王對他説。"我還沒巡視過我的王國。我太老了，我沒地方放馬車，走路又累得慌。"

"噢！可是我已經看過了，"小王子説着，又朝這顆小行星的另一邊瞥了一眼。

"那邊也沒有一個人……"

"那你就審判你自己，"國王回答他説。"這是最難的。審判自己要比審判別人難得多。要是你能審判好自己，你就是個真正的智者。"

"可是我，"小王子説，"我在哪裏都可以自己審判自己。我不必留在這裏呀。"

"嗯！嗯！"國王説，"我想哪，在我的星球上是有隻老鼠。夜裏我聽見牠的聲音。你可以審判這隻老鼠。你可以不時判牠死刑。這樣啊，牠的生命就取決於你的判決了。不過，這隻老鼠你必須省下來用，每次判決後都必須赦免牠。因為只有這麼一隻老鼠。"

"可是我，"小王子回答説，"我不喜歡判死刑，我想我還是必須走。"

"不行，"國王説。

整裝待發的小王子不想讓老國王難過：

"陛下如果想讓命令立刻得到服從，那就不妨下一道合情合理的命令。比如説，陛下可以命令我在一分鐘內離開此地。我覺得條件已經成熟……”

　　國王一聲不響，小王子起先有點猶豫，而後歎了口氣，就起程了。

　　“我任命你當我的大使，”這時國王趕緊喊道。

　　他的神態威嚴極了。

　　“這些大人真奇怪，”小王子在旅途中自言自語地説。

第十一章

第二顆行星上住着一個愛虛榮的人。

"哈哈！有個崇拜者來看我了！"這個愛虛榮的人剛看見小王子，大老遠就喊了起來。

因為，在愛虛榮的人眼裏，別人都是他們的崇拜者。

"您好，"小王子說。"您這頂帽子挺有趣的。"

"這是用來致意的，"愛虛榮的人回答說，"人家向我歡呼時，我就用帽子向他們致意。可惜啊，一直沒人經過這裏。"

"是嗎？"小王子說，他沒明白那人的意思。

"你用一隻手去拍另一隻手，"於是愛虛榮的人這樣教他。

小王子就拍起手掌來了。愛虛榮的人抬起帽子，謙遜地致意。

"這比拜訪那個國王好玩多了，"小王子心想。他又拍起手掌來了。愛虛榮的人就又抬起帽子致意。

這樣玩了五分鐘，小王子覺得太單調，他都玩累了：

"要想叫這頂帽子掉下來，該怎麼做呢？"

可是愛虛榮的人沒聽見他的話。愛虛榮的人只聽得見頌揚的話。

"你真的很崇拜我嗎？"他問小王子。

"崇拜是甚麼意思？"

"崇拜的意思就是，承認我是這個星球上最英俊、最時髦、最富有、最有學問的人。"

"可是這個星球上只有你一個人呀！"

"幫幫忙。你只管崇拜我就是了！"

"我崇拜你，"小王子說着，微微聳了聳肩膀，"可是你要這個做甚麼呢？"說着，小王子就走開了。

"這些大人真的很怪喲，"一路上，他這麼對自己說了一句。

第十二章

下一顆行星上住着一個酒鬼。這次探訪時間很短，卻使小王子陷入了深深的悵惘之中。

他看見那個酒鬼靜靜地坐在桌前，面前有一堆空酒瓶和一堆裝得滿滿的酒瓶，他就問："你在那裏做甚麼呢？"

"我喝酒，"酒鬼神情悲傷地回答。

"你為甚麼要喝酒呢？"小王子問。

"為了忘記，"酒鬼回答。

"忘記甚麼？"小王子已經有些同情他了。

"忘記我的羞愧，"酒鬼垂下腦袋坦白説。

"為甚麼感到羞愧？"小王子又問，他想幫助這個人。

"為喝酒感到羞愧！"酒鬼説完這句話，就再也不開口了。

小王子茫然不解地走了。

"這些大人真的很怪很怪，"一路上，他自言自語地説。

第十三章

第四顆行星是個商人的星球。這個人實在太忙碌了，看見小王子來，連頭也沒抬一下。

"您好，"小王子對他說，"您的煙卷滅了。"

"三加二等於五。五加七等於十二。十二加三等於十五。你好。十五加七等於二十二。二十二加六是二十八。沒時間再去點着它。二十六加五，三十一。啊哈！一共是五億一百六十二萬二千七百三十一。"

"五億甚麼呀？"

"啊？你還在這裏？五億一百萬……我也不知道是甚麼……我的工作太多了！我做的都是正事，我沒有時間閒聊！二加五等於七……"

"五億一百萬甚麼？"小王子又問一遍，他向來是不提問題則罷，提了就決不放過。

商人抬起頭來：

"我在這個星球上住了五十四個年頭，只被打攪過三次。第一次是二十二年以前，有隻不知從哪裏跑來的金龜子，弄出一片可怕的聲音，害得我在一筆賬目裏出了四個差錯。第二次是十一年前，我風濕病發作。我平時缺乏鍛煉。我沒時間去閒逛。我是做正事的人。第三次……就是這次！所以我剛才説了，五億一百萬……"

"五億一百萬甚麼？"

商人明白他是別想有安寧的日子了：

"五億一百萬個小東西，有時候在天空裏看得見它們。"

"蒼蠅？"

"不對，是閃閃發亮的小東西。"

"蜜蜂？"

"不對。是些金色的小東西，無所事事的人望着它們會胡思亂想。可我是做正事的人！我沒時間去胡思亂想。"

"噢！是星星？"

"對啦。星星。"

"你拿這五億顆星星做甚麼呢？"

"五億一百六十二萬二千七百三十一顆。我是個認真的人，我講究精確。"

"那你拿這些星星來做甚麼呢？"

"我拿它們做甚麼？"

"是啊。"

"不做甚麼。我佔有它們。"

"你佔有這些星星？"

"對。"

"可是我已經見到有個國王，他……"

"國王並不佔有。他們只是'統治'。這完全是兩回事。"

"佔有這些星星對你有甚麼用呢？"

"可以使我富有。"

"富有對你有甚麼用呢？"

"可以去買其他的星星──只要有人發現了這樣的星星。"

"這個人，"小王子暗自思忖，"想問題有點像那個酒鬼。"

話雖這麼說，他還是接着提問題：

"一個人怎麼能夠佔有這些星星呢？"

"它們屬於誰了？"商人沒好氣地頂了他一句。

"我不知道。誰也不屬於。"

"那麼它們就屬於我，因為是我第一個想到這件事的。"

"這就夠了？"

"當然。當你發現一顆不屬於任何人的鑽石，它就屬於你。當你發現一個不屬於任何人的島嶼，它就屬於你。當你最先想出一個主意，你去申請發明專利，它就屬於你。現在我佔有了這些星星，因為在我以前沒有人想到過佔有它們。"

"這倒也是，"小王子說，"可你拿它們來做甚麼呢？"

"我經營它們。我一遍又一遍地計算它們的數目，"商人說，"這並不容易。但我是個做正事的人！"

小王子還是不滿意。

"我呀，如果我有一塊方圍巾，我可以把它圍在頸項上帶走它。如果我有一朵花兒，我可以摘下這朵花兒帶走它。可是你沒法摘下這些星星呀！"

"沒錯，但是我可以把它們存入銀行。"

"這是甚麼意思？"

"這就是說，我把我的星星的總數寫在一張小紙片上。然後我把這張小紙片放進一個抽屜鎖好。"

"就這些？"

"這就夠了！"

"真有趣，"小王子心想，"倒挺有詩意的。可這算不上甚麼正事呀。"

小王子對正事的看法，跟大人對正事的看法很不相同。

"我有一朵花兒，"他又說道，"我每天都給她澆水。我有三座火山，我每星期都把它們疏通一遍。那座死火山我也疏通。因為誰也說不定它還會不會噴發。我佔有它們，對火山有好處，對花兒也有好處。可是你佔有星星，對它們沒有好處。"商人張口結舌，無言以對。小王子就走了。

"這些大人真的好古怪，"一路上，他只是自言自語說了這麼一句。

第十四章

第五顆行星非常奇怪。這是最小的一顆。上面剛好只能容得下一盞路燈和一個點燈人。小王子好生納悶，在天空的一個角落，在一個既沒有房子也沒有居民的行星上，要一盞路燈和一個點燈人，又能有甚麼用呢？不過他還是對自己說：

"很可能這個人是有點不正常。但是跟那個國王，那個愛虛榮的人，那個商人和那個酒鬼比起來，他還是要比他們正常些。至少他的工作還有意義。他點亮路燈，就好比喚醒了另一個太陽或者一朵花兒。他熄滅路燈，就好比讓這朵花兒或這個太陽睡覺了。這是件很美的事情。既然很美，自然就有用！"

他一到這個星球，就很尊敬地向點燈人打招呼：

"早上好。你剛才為甚麼熄掉路燈呢？"

"這是規定，"點燈人回答說，"早上好。"

"甚麼規定？"

"熄滅路燈囉。晚上好。"

說着他又點亮了路燈。

"那你剛才為甚麼又點亮路燈呢？"

"這是規定，"點燈人回答說。

"我弄不懂，"小王子說。

"沒甚麼要弄懂的，"點燈人說，"規定就是規定。早上好。"

說着他熄滅了路燈。

然後他用一塊有紅方格的手帕擦了擦額頭。

"我做的是件非常累人的差事。以前還說得過去。我早晨熄燈，晚上點燈。白天我有時間休息，夜裏也有時間睡覺……"

"那麼，後來規定改變了？"

"規定沒有改變，"點燈人說，"慘就慘在這裏！這顆行星一年比一年轉得快，可是規定卻沒變！"

"結果呢？"小王子說。

"結果現在每分鐘轉一圈，我連一秒鐘的休息時間都沒有。我每分鐘就要點一次燈，熄一次燈！"

"這可真有趣！你這裏一天只有一分鐘！"

"一點也不有趣，"點燈人說，"我們說着話，就已經一個月過去了。"

“一個月？”

“對。三十分鐘。三十天！晚上好。”

說着他點亮了路燈。

小王子看着他，心裏喜歡上了這個忠於職守的點燈人。他想起了自己以前移動椅子看日落。他挺想幫助這個朋友：

“你知道……我有一個辦法，好讓你想休息就能休息……”

“我一直想休息，”點燈人説。

因為，一個人可以同時是忠於職守的，又是生性疏懶的。

小王子接着説：

“你的星球小得很，你走三步就繞了一圈。所以你只要走得慢一些，就可以一直留在陽光下。你要想休息了，就往前走……你要白天有多長，它就有多長。”

“這辦法幫不了我多少忙，”點燈人説，“我這人，平生就喜歡睡覺。”

“真不走運，”小王子説。

“真不走運，”點燈人説，“早上好。”

說着他熄滅了路燈。

“這個人呀，”小王子一邊繼續他的旅途，一邊在想，“國王也好，愛虛榮的人也好，酒鬼也好，商人也好，他們都會看不起這個人。可是，就只有他沒讓我感到可笑。也許，這是因為他關心的是別的事情，而不是自己。”

他惋惜地歎了口氣，又自言自語：

"只有這個人我可以跟他交朋友。可是他的星球實在太小了。兩個人擠不下⋯⋯"

小王子不敢承認的是，他留戀這顆受上蒼眷顧的星球，是因為每二十四小時就有一千四百四十次日落！

第十五章

第六顆行星是一顆大十倍的行星。上面住着一個老先生，他在寫一本大部頭的著作。

"看！來了一位探險家！"他一看見小王子，就喊道。

小王子坐在桌邊，喘了喘氣。他剛走了那麼多路！

"你從哪裏來啊？"老先生問他。

"這一大本是甚麼書？"小王子説，"您在這裏做甚麼呢？"

"我是地理學家，"老先生説。

"甚麼叫地理學家？"

"地理學家是個學者，他知道哪裏有海洋，有河流，有城市，有山脈和沙漠。"

"這挺有趣，"小王子説，"啊，這才是真正的職業！"説着他朝地理學家的星球四周望了一眼。他還從沒見過這麼雄偉壯麗的星球呢。

"您的星球真美。它有海洋嗎？"

"這我沒法知道，"地理學家説。

"哦！"小王子有點失望。"那麼山脈呢？"

"這我沒法知道，"地理學家説。

"城市、河流和沙漠呢？"

"這我也沒法知道，"地理學家説。

"但您是地理學家呀！"

"一點不錯，"地理學家説，"但我不是探險家。我這裏一個探險家也沒有。地理學家是不出去探測城市、河流、山脈、海洋和沙漠的。地理學家非常重要，他不能到處閒逛。他從不離開自己的書房。不過他會在那裏接見探險家。他向他們提問，把他們的旅行回憶記下來。要是他覺得他們中間哪個人的回憶有意思，他就會讓人對這個探險家的品行作一番調查。"

"這是為甚麼？"

"因為一個説謊的探險家會給地理書帶來災難性的後果。一個貪杯的探險家也是如此。"

"這是為甚麼？"小王子問。

"因為酒鬼會把一樣東西看成兩樣東西。這樣一來，地理學家就會把明明只有一座山的地方寫成有兩座山了。"

"我認識一個人，"小王子説，"他當探險家就不行。"

"這有可能。所以，要等到了解探險家品行良好以後，才對他的發現進行調查。"

"去看一下？"

"不。這太複雜了。地理學家只要求探險家提供物證。比如說，他發現了一座大山，地理學家就要求他帶一塊大石頭來。"

地理學家忽然激動起來。

"嗨，你是大老遠來的！你是探險家！你給我說說你的星球！"

說着，地理學家打開筆記本，削了支鉛筆。地理學家一開始只用鉛筆記下探險家講的話。要等到這個探險家提供物證以後，才換用鋼筆來記錄。

"怎麼樣？"地理學家問。

"哦！我那裏，"小王子說，"並不很有趣，那是顆很小的星球。我有三座火山。兩座活火山，一座死火山。不過這也說不定。"

"這可說不定，"地理學家說。

"我還有一朵花兒。"

"花兒我們是不記下來的，"地理學家說。

"這是為甚麼？花兒是最美的呀！"

"因為花是轉瞬即逝的。"

"甚麼叫'轉瞬即逝'呢？"

"地理書，"地理學家說，"是所有的書中間最寶貴的。

地理書永遠不會過時。山脈移位的情形是極其罕見的。海洋乾涸的情形也是極其罕見的。我們寫的都是永恆的事物。"

"可是死火山說不定也會醒來,"小王子插話說,"甚麼叫'轉瞬即逝'呢?"

"火山睡也好,醒也好,對我們地理學家來說是一回事,"地理學家說,"我們關心的是山。山是一成不變的。"

"可是,甚麼叫'轉瞬即逝'呢?"小王子追問道,他向來提了問題就不肯放過。

"意思就是'隨時有消逝的危險'。"

"我的花兒隨時有消逝的危險嗎?"

"當然。"

"我的花兒是轉瞬即逝的,"小王子想道,"她只有四根刺可以自衛,可以用來抵禦這個世界!而我卻丟下她孤零零地在那裏!"

想到這裏,他不由得感到了後悔。不過他馬上又振作起來:

"依您看,我再去哪裏探訪好呢?"他問。

"地球吧,"地理學家回答說,"它的名氣頗響……"

於是小王子走了,一邊走一邊想着他的花兒。

第十六章

所以，第七顆行星就是地球了。

地球可不是普普通通的行星！它上面有一百一十一個國王（當然，黑人國王也包括在內），七千萬個地理學家，九十萬個商人，七百五十萬個酒鬼，三億一千一百個愛虛榮的人，總共大約有二十億個大人。

為了讓你們對地球的大小有個概念，我就這麼對你們說吧，在發明電以前，地球的六大洲上，需要維持一支四十六萬二千五百一十一人的浩浩蕩蕩的點燈人大軍。

從稍遠些的地方看去，這是一幅壯麗的景觀。這支大軍行動起來，就像在歌劇院裏跳芭蕾舞那樣有條不紊。最先上場的是新西蘭和澳大利亞的點燈人。點着了燈，他們就退下去睡覺。接着是中國和西伯利亞的點燈人上場，隨後他們也退到幕後。下面輪到了俄羅斯和印度的點燈人。接下去是非洲和歐洲的，而後是南美的。再後來是北美的。所有這些點燈人從來不會搞亂上場的次序。這場面真是蔚為壯觀。

　　只有北極（那裏只有惟一一盞路燈）的點燈人和南極（那裏也只有惟一一盞路燈）的那個同行，過着悠閒懶散的生活：他們一年工作兩次。

第十七章

　　個人如果想把話說得有趣些，免不了會稍稍撒點謊。

　　我給你們講點燈人大軍的那一會，就不是很誠實。那些不了解我們行星的人，聽了我講的故事，可能會造成一種錯覺。其實人在地球上只佔一點點地方。倘若讓地球上的二十億居民全都挨在一起站着，就像集會時那樣，那麼二十海里長、二十海里寬的一個廣場就容得下他們。全人類可以擠在太平洋中最小的一個島嶼上。

　　當然，大人是不會相信你們的。他們自以為佔了很多很多地方。他們把自己看得跟猴麵包樹一樣重要。你們不妨勸他們好好算一算。他們喜歡數字，說到計算就很振奮。不過你們別浪費時間去做這種叫人厭煩的事情。根本不用去做。你們相信我就行了。

　　所以小王子一踏上地球，就覺得奇怪，怎麼一個人也看不見呢。他正在擔心是不是來錯了星球，忽然看見沙地上一個月白色的圓環在移動。

"晚上好，"小王子沒把握地招呼說。

"晚上好，"蛇說。

"我落在哪個行星上了？"小王子問。

"在地球上，這是非洲，"蛇回答。

"噢！難道地球上一個人也沒有嗎？"

"這裏是沙漠。在沙漠裏是一個人也沒有的。地球大得很，"蛇說。

小王子在一塊石頭上坐下，抬頭望着天空：

"我在想，"他說，"這些星星閃閃發亮，大概是要讓每個人總有一天能找到自己的那顆星星吧。看我的那顆星星。它正好在我們頭頂上……可是它離得那麼遠！"

"它很美，"蛇說，"你到這裏來做甚麼呢？"

"我和一朵花兒鬧了意見，"小王子說。

"噢！"蛇說。

他們兩個都沉默了。

"哪裏見得到人呢？"小王子終於又開口了，"在沙漠裏真有點孤獨……"

"在人群中間，你也會感到孤獨，"蛇說。

小王子久久地注視着蛇：

"你真是種奇怪的動物，"最後他說，"細得像根手指……"

"可是我比一個國王的手指還厲害呢，"蛇説。

小王子笑了：

"你厲害不到哪裏去……你連腳都沒有……要出遠門你就不行吧？"

"我可以把你帶到很遠很遠的地方去，比一艘船去的地方還遠，"蛇説。

牠盤在小王子的腳踝上，像一隻金鐲子：

"凡是我碰過的人，我都把他們送回老家去，"牠又説，"但你這麼純潔，又是從一顆星星那裏來的……"

小王子沒有作聲。

"在這個花崗石的地球上，你是這麼弱小，我很可憐你。哪天你要是想念你的星星了，我可以幫助你。我可以……"

"噢！我明白你的意思，"小王子説，"可是為甚麼你説的話都像謎似的？"

"這些謎我都能解開，"蛇説。

然後他們又都沉默了。

第十八章

小王子穿過沙漠，只見到了一朵花兒。一朵長着三片花瓣的花兒，一朵不起眼的花兒……

"你好，"小王子説。

"你好，"花兒説。

"人們在哪裏呢？"小王子有禮貌地問。

花兒看見過一支沙漠駝隊經過：

"人們？我想是有的，不是六個就是七個。好幾年以前，我見過他們。不過誰也不知道，要上哪裏才能找到他們。風把他們這一會吹到這裏，那一會吹到那裏。他們沒有根，活得很辛苦。"

"再見了，"小王子説。

"再見，"花兒説。

第十九章

小王子攀上一座高山。他過去只見過三座齊膝高的火山。他還把那座死火山當櫈子坐呢。"從一座這麼高的山上望下去,"他心想,"我一眼就能看到整個星球和所有的人們……"可是,他看到的只是些陡峭的山峰。

"你們好,"他怯生生地招呼說。

"你們好……你們好……你們好……"回聲應道。

"你們是誰呀?"小王子問。

"你們是誰呀……你們是誰呀……你們是誰呀……"回聲應道。

"請做我的朋友吧,我很孤獨,"他說。

"我很孤獨……我很孤獨……我很孤獨……"回聲應道。

"這顆行星可真怪!"他心想,"又乾,又尖,又鋒利。人們一點想像力都沒有。他們老是重複別人對他們說的話……在我那裏有一朵花兒,她總是先開口說話的……"

第二十章

小王子在沙漠、山岩和雪地上走了很長時間以後，終於發現了一條路。所有的路都通往有人住的地方。

"你們好，"他説。

眼前是一個玫瑰盛開的花園。

"你好，"玫瑰們説。

小王子看着她們。她們都長得和他的花兒一模一樣。

"你們是甚麼花呀？"他驚奇地問。

"我們是玫瑰花，"玫瑰們説。

"噢！"小王子説⋯⋯

他感到非常傷心。他的花兒跟他説過，她是整個宇宙中獨一無二的花兒。但這裏，在一個花園裏就有五千朵，全都一模一樣！

"要是讓她看到了，"他想，"她一定會非常生氣⋯⋯她會拼命咳嗽，她還會假裝死去，免得被人恥笑。我呢，還必須假裝去照料她，否則她為了讓我感到羞愧，説不定真的會讓自己死去……"

　　隨後他又想："我還以為自己擁有的是獨一無二的一朵花兒呢，但我有的只是普普通通的一朵玫瑰花罷了。這朵花兒，加上那三座只到我膝蓋的火山，其中有一座還説不定永遠不會再噴發，就憑這些，我怎麼也成不了一個偉大的王子……" 想着想着，他趴在草地上哭了起來。

第二十一章

就在這時狐狸出現了。

"早哇，"狐狸説。

"早，"小王子有禮貌地回答，他轉過身來，卻甚麼也沒看到。

"我在這裏呢，"那聲音説，"在蘋果樹下面……"

"你是誰？"小王子説，"你很漂亮。"

"我是一隻狐狸，"狐狸説。

"來和我一起玩吧，"小王子提議，"我很不快活……"

"我不能和你一起玩，"狐狸説，"還沒人馴養過我呢。"

"啊！對不起，"小王子説。

不過，他想了想又説：

"'馴養'是甚麼意思？"

"你一定不是這裏的人，"狐狸説，"你來尋找甚麼呢？"

"我來找人，"小王子説。"'馴養'是甚麼意思？"

"人哪，"狐狸説，"他們有槍，還打獵。討厭極了！他們還養母雞，這總算有點意思。你也找母雞嗎？"

"不找，"小王子説。"我找朋友。'馴養'是甚麼意思？"

"這是一件經常被忽略的事情，"狐狸説。"意思是'建立感情聯繫'……"

"建立感情聯繫？"

"當然，"狐狸説，"現在你對我來説，只不過是個小男孩，跟成千上萬別的小男孩毫無兩樣。我不需要你。你也不需要我。我對你來説，也只不過是隻狐狸，跟成千上萬別的狐狸毫無兩樣。但是，你要是馴養了我，我倆就彼此都需要對方了。你對我來説是世界上獨一無二的。我對你來説，也是世界上獨一無二的……"

"我有點明白了，"小王子説，"有一朵花兒……我想她是馴養了我……"

"有可能，"狐狸説，"這個地球上各種各樣的事都有……"

"哦！不是在地球上，"小王子説。

狐狸看上去很驚訝：

"在另一個星球上？"

"對。"

"在那個星球上有沒有獵人呢？"

"沒有。"

“哈，這很有意思！那麼母雞呢？”

“沒有。”

“沒有十全十美的事呵，”狐狸歎氣説。

不過，狐狸很快又回到剛才的想法上來：

“我的生活很單調。我去捉雞，人來捉我。母雞全都長得一個模樣，人也全都長得一個模樣。所以我有點膩了。不過，要是你馴養我，我的生活就會變得充滿陽光。我會辨認出一種和其他所有人都不同的腳步聲。聽見別的腳步聲，我會往地底下鑽，而你的腳步聲，會像音樂一樣，把我召喚到洞外。還有，你看！你看到那邊的麥田了嗎？我是不吃麵包的。麥子對我來說毫無用處。我對麥田無動於衷。可悲就可悲在這裏！而你的頭髮是金黃色的。所以，一旦你馴養了我，事情就變得很美妙了！金黃色的麥子，會讓我想起你。我會喜愛風吹拂麥浪的聲音……”

狐狸停下來，久久地注視着小王子：

“請你……馴養我吧！”牠説。

“我很願意，”小王子回答説，“可是我時間不多了。我必須去找朋友，還須去了解許多東西。”

“只有馴養過的東西，你才會了解牠，”狐狸説，“人們也沒有時間去了解任何東西。他們總到商店去購買現成的東西。但是不存在出售朋友的商店，所以人們也就不會有朋友。你如果想要有個朋友，就馴養我吧！”

"那麼應當做些甚麼呢？"小王子説。

"應當很有耐心，"狐狸回答説，"你先坐在草地上，離我稍遠一些，就像這樣。我從眼角裏瞅你，而你甚麼也別説。語言是誤解的根源。不過，每天你都可以坐得離我稍稍近一些……"

第二天，小王子又來了。

"最好你能在同一時間來，"狐狸説，"比如説，下午四點鐘吧，那麼我在三點鐘就會開始感到幸福了。時間越來越近，我就越來越幸福。到了四點鐘，我會興奮得坐立不安；幸福原來也很折磨人的！但要是你隨便甚麼時候來，我就沒法知道甚麼時候該準備好我的心情……還是必須有個儀式。"

"甚麼叫儀式？"小王子問。

"這也是一件經常被忽略的事情，"狐狸説，"就是定下一個日子，使它不同於其他的日子，定下一個時間，使它不同於其他的時間。比如説，獵人有一種儀式。每星期四他們都和村裏的女孩子跳舞。所以呢，星期四就是個美妙的日子！這一天我總要到葡萄地裏去轉一轉。要是獵人們隨時跳舞，每天不就都一模一樣，我不也就沒有假期了嗎？"

就這樣，小王子馴養了狐狸。而後，眼看分手的時刻臨近了：

"哎！"狐狸説，"……我要哭了。"

"這可是你的不是喲，"小王子説，"我本來沒想讓你受任何傷害，可你卻要我馴養你……"

"可不是，"狐狸説。

"不過你要哭了！"小王子説。

"可不是，"狐狸説。

"結果你甚麼好處也沒得到！"

"我得到了，"狐狸説，"是麥田的顏色給我的。"

他隨即又説：

"你再去看看那些玫瑰花吧。你會明白你那朵玫瑰是世界上獨一無二的。然後你再回來跟我告別，我要告訴你一個秘密作為臨別禮物。"

小王子就去看那些玫瑰。

"你們根本不像我那朵玫瑰，你們還甚麼都不是呢，"他對她們説，"誰都沒馴養過你們，你們也誰都沒馴養過。你們就像狐狸以前一樣。那時候的牠，和成千上萬別的狐狸毫無兩樣。可是我現在和牠做了朋友，牠在世界上就是獨一無二的了。"

玫瑰們都很難為情。

"你們很美，但你們是空虛的，"小王子接着説，"沒有人能為你們去死。當然，我那朵玫瑰在一個過路人眼裏跟你們也一樣。然而對於我來説，單單她這一朵，就比你們全體都重要得多。因為我給她澆過水，我給她蓋過罩子，我給她遮過風障，我給她除過毛蟲的（只把兩三條要變成蝴蝶的留下）。我聽她抱怨和自詡，有時也和她默默相對。她，是我的玫瑰。"

說完，他又回到狐狸跟前：

"再見了⋯⋯"他說。

"再見，"狐狸說，"我告訴你那個秘密，它很簡單：只有用心才能看見。本質的東西用眼是看不見的。"

"本質的東西用眼是看不見的，"小王子重複了一遍，他要記住這句話。

"正是你為你的玫瑰花費的時光，才使你的玫瑰變得如此重要。"

"正是我為我的玫瑰花費的時光，才使我的玫瑰變得如此重要，"小王子說，他要記住這句話。

"人們已經忘記了這個道理，"狐狸說。"但你不該忘記它。對你馴養過的東西，你永遠負有責任。你必須對你的玫瑰負責⋯⋯"

"我必須對我的玫瑰負責⋯⋯"小王子重複一遍，他要記住這句話。

第二十二章

“你好，”小王子説。

“你好，”扳道工説。

“你在這裏做甚麼？”小王子問。

“我在分送旅客，一千人一撥，”扳道工説，“我發送運載旅客的列車，一會往右，一會往左。”

説着，一列燈火通明的快車，像打雷似的轟鳴着駛過，震得扳道房直打顫。

“他們好匆忙，”小王子説，“他們去找甚麼呢？”

“開火車的人自己也不知道，”扳道工説。

説話間，又一列燈火通明的快車，朝相反的方向轟鳴而去。

“他們已經回來了？”小王子問。

“不是剛才的那列，”扳道工説，“這是對開列車。”

“他們對原來的地方不滿意嗎？”

"人們對自己的地方從來不會滿意，"扳道工説。

第三列燈火通明的快車轟鳴着駛過。

"他們是去追趕第一批旅客嗎？"小王子問。

"他們沒追趕誰，"扳道工説，"他們在裏面睡覺，或者打哈欠。只有孩子把鼻子貼在窗上看外面。"

"只有孩子知道自己在找甚麼，"小王子説，"他們在一個布娃娃身上花了好些時間，她對他們來説就成了很重要的東西。要是有人奪走他們的布娃娃，他們會哭的……"

"他們真幸運，"扳道工説。

第二十三章

“你好，”小王子說。

“你好，”商人説。

他是個賣複方止渴丸的商人。每星期只要吞服一粒，就不會感到口渴了。

“你為甚麼要賣這東西？”小王子問。

“它可以大大節約時間，”商人説，“專家做過計算。每星期可以省下五十三分鐘。”

“省下的五十三分鐘有甚麼用呢？”

“隨便怎麼用都行⋯⋯”

“我呀，”小王子心想，“要是我省下這五十三分鐘，我就不慌不忙地朝泉水走去⋯⋯”

第二十四章

這是我降落在沙漠後的第八天，我聽着這個商人的故事，喝完了最後一滴備用水。

"喔！"我對小王子説，"你的回憶很動人，可是我飛機還沒修好，水也喝完了，要是我能朝泉水走去，那真是有福了！"

"我那狐狸朋友⋯⋯"他説。

"小傢伙，這可不關狐狸的事！"

"為甚麼？"

"因為我快要渴死了⋯⋯"

他沒明白我的思路，回答我説：

"有朋友真好，即使就要死了，我也還是這麼想。我真高興，有過一隻狐狸作為朋友⋯⋯"

"他沒明白情勢有多凶險，"我心想，"他從來不知道飢渴。只要有點陽光，他就足夠了⋯⋯"

然而他注視着我，好像知道我心裏在想甚麼：

"我也渴……我們去找一口井吧……"

我做了個表示厭煩的手勢：在一望無垠的沙漠中，漫無目標地去找井，簡直是荒唐。然而，我們到底還是上路了。

默默地走了幾個鐘頭以後，夜幕降臨了，星星在天空中閃爍起來。由於渴得厲害，我有點發燒，望着天上的星星，彷彿在夢中。小王子的話在腦海裏盤旋舞蹈。

"你也渴？"我問。

他沒有回答我的問題，只對我説：

"水對心靈也有好處……"

我沒聽懂他的話，但我沒作聲……我知道，這一會不該去問他。

他累了。他坐了下來。我坐在他身旁。沉默了一會，他又説：

"星星很美，因為有一朵看不見的花兒……"

我説了聲"可不是"，就靜靜地注視着月光下沙漠的褶皺。

"沙漠很美，"他又説。

沒錯。我一向喜歡沙漠。我們坐在一個沙丘上。甚麼也看不見。甚麼也聽不見。然而有甚麼東西在寂靜中發出光芒……

"沙漠這麼美，"小王子説，"是因為有個地方藏着一口井……"

我非常吃驚，突然間明白了沙漠發光的奧秘。我小時候住在一座老宅裏，傳說宅裏埋着寶藏。當然，從來沒人發現過這寶藏，或許根本沒人尋找過它。但是它使整座老宅變得令人着迷。我的老宅在心靈深處藏着一個秘密……

"對，"我對小王子説，"不管是老宅，還是星星或沙漠，使它們變美的東西，都是看不見的！"

"我很高興，"他説，"你和狐狸的看法一樣了。"

看小王子睡着了，我把他抱起來，重新上路。我很激動。我覺得就像捧着一件易碎的寶貝。我甚至覺得在地球上，再沒有更嬌弱的東西了。我在月光下看着他蒼白的前額，緊閉的眼睛，還有那隨風飄動的髮綹，在心裏對自己説："我所看到的只是外貌。最重要的東西是看不見的……"

當他微微張開的嘴唇綻出一絲笑意時，我又對自己説："在這個熟睡的小王子身上，最讓我感動的，是他對一朵花兒的忠貞，這朵玫瑰的影像，即使在他睡着時，仍然在他身上發出光芒，就像一盞燈的火焰一樣……"這時我把他想得更加嬌弱了。應該好好保護燈火呵，一陣風就會吹滅它……

就這樣走啊走啊，我在拂曉時發現了水井。

第二十五章

"人們擠進快車,"小王子説,"可是又不知道還要去尋找甚麼。所以他們忙忙碌碌,轉來轉去⋯⋯"

他接着又説:

"其實何必呢⋯⋯"

我們找到的這口井,跟撒哈拉沙漠的那些井不一樣。那些井,只是沙漠上挖的洞而已。這口井很像村莊裏的那種井。可是這裏根本就沒有村莊呀,我覺得自己在做夢。

"真奇怪,"我對小王子説,"樣樣都是現成的:轆轤、水桶、吊繩⋯⋯"

他笑了,拉住吊繩,讓轆轤轉起來。轆轤咕咕作響,就像一隻吹不到風、沉睡已久的舊風標發出的聲音。

"你聽見嗎,"小王子説,"我們喚醒了這口井,它在唱歌呢⋯⋯"

我不想讓他多用力氣:

"讓我來吧，"我說，"這工作對你來說太重了。"

我把水桶緩緩地吊到井欄上，穩穩地擱住。轆轤的歌聲還在耳邊響着，而在依然晃動着的水面上，我看見太陽在晃動。

"我想喝水，"小王子說，"給我喝吧……"

我這時明白了他在尋找的是甚麼！

我把水桶舉到他的嘴邊。他喝着水，眼睛沒張開。水像節日一般美好。它已經不只是一種維持生命的物質。它來自星光下的跋涉，來自轆轤的歌唱，來自臂膀的用力。它像禮物一樣愉悦着心靈。當我是個小男孩時，聖誕樹的燈光，午夜彌撒的音樂，人們甜蜜的微笑，都曾像這樣輝映着我收到的聖誕禮物，讓它熠熠發光。

"你這裏的人，"小王子說，"在一個花園裏種出五千朵玫瑰，卻沒能從中找到自己要找的東西……"

"他們是沒能找到……"我應聲說。

"然而他們要找的東西，在一朵玫瑰或者一點水裏就能找到……"

"可不是，"我應聲說。

小王子接着說：

"但是用眼是看不見的。必須用心去找。"

我喝了水。我痛快地呼吸着空氣。沙漠在晨曦中泛出蜂蜜的色澤。這種蜂蜜的色澤，也使我心頭洋溢着幸福的感覺。我為甚麼要難過呢⋯⋯

"你該實踐自己的諾言了，"小王子柔聲對我說，他這一
會又坐在了我的身邊。

"甚麼諾言？"

"你知道的⋯⋯給我的羊畫個嘴罩⋯⋯我要對我的花兒
負責！"

我從衣袋裏掏出幾幅畫稿。小王子瞥了一眼，笑着說：

"你的猴麵包樹呀，有點像白菜⋯⋯"

"哦！"

可是我還為這幾棵猴麵包樹感到挺得意呢！

"你的狐狸⋯⋯牠的耳朵⋯⋯有點像兩隻角⋯⋯再說也
太長了！"

說着他又笑了起來。

"你不公平，小傢伙，我可就畫過剖開和不剖開的蟒蛇，
別的都沒學過。"

"噢！這就行了，"他說，"孩子們會看懂的。"

我用鉛筆畫了一隻嘴罩。把畫遞給他時，我的心揪緊
了：

"你有些甚麼打算，我都不知道⋯⋯"

但他沒回答，卻對我說：

"你知道，我降落到地球上⋯⋯到明天就滿一年了⋯⋯"

然後，一陣靜默過後，他又說道：

"我就落在這裏附近⋯⋯"

說着他的臉紅了起來。

我也不知是甚麼原因，只覺得又感到一陣異樣的憂傷。可是我想到了一個問題：

"這麼說，一星期前我遇見你的那個早晨，你獨自在這片荒無人煙的沙漠裏走來，並不是偶然的了？你是要回到當初降落的地方去吧？"

小王子的臉又紅了。

我有些猶豫地接着說：

"也許，是為了週年紀念？⋯⋯"

小王子臉又紅了。他往往不回答人家的問題，但他臉一紅，就等於在說"對的"，可不是嗎？

"哎！"我對他說，"我怕⋯⋯"

他卻回答我說：

"現在你該去工作了。你必須回到你的飛機那裏去。我在這裏等你。明天晚上再來吧⋯⋯"

可是我放心不下。我想起了狐狸的話。一個人要是被馴養過，恐怕難免要哭的⋯⋯

第二十六章

在水井邊上，有一堵殘敗的舊石牆。第二天傍晚，我工作後回來，遠遠地看見小王子兩腿懸空地坐在斷牆上。我還聽見他在說話：

"難道你不記得了？"他說。"根本不是這裏！"

想必有一個聲音在回答他，只見他在反駁：

"對！對！是今天，可不是這個地方……"

我往石牆走去。我既沒看見人影，也沒聽見人聲。但是小王子又在說：

"……那當然。在沙地上，你會看到我的足跡是從哪裏開始的。你只要等着我就行了。今天夜裏我就去那裏。"

我離石牆只有二十米了，可還是甚麼也沒看見。

停了一會，小王子又說道：

"你的毒液管用嗎？你有把握不會讓我難受很久嗎？"

我心頭猛地揪緊，停下了腳步，可是我還是甚麼也不明白。

“現在，來吧，”小王子説，“……我要下來了！”

這時，我低頭朝牆腳看去，不由得嚇了一跳！只見一條半分鐘就能叫人致命的黃蛇，昂然豎起身子對着小王子。我一邊伸手去掏手槍，一邊撒腿往前奔去。可是，那條蛇聽見我的聲音，就像一條水柱驟然跌落下來，緩緩滲入沙地，不慌不忙地鑽進石縫中去，發出輕微的金屬聲。

我趕到牆邊，正好接住從牆上跳下的小王子，把這個臉色白得像雪的小傢伙抱在懷裏。

“這是怎麼回事！你居然跟蛇在談話！”

我解開他一直戴着的金黃色圍巾。我用水沾濕他的太陽穴，給他喝了點水。可是此刻我不敢再問他甚麼。他神色凝重地望着我，用雙臂摟住我的頸項。我感覺到他的心跳，就像被槍彈擊中瀕臨死亡的小鳥的心跳。他對我説：

“我很高興，你找到了飛機上缺少的東西。你可以回家了……”

“你怎麼知道的？”

我正想告訴他，就在剛才，在眼看沒有希望的情況下，我修好了飛機！

他沒回答我的問題，但接着説：

“我也一樣，今天，我要回家了……”

然後，憂鬱地説：

“那要遠得多……難得多……”

我意識到發生了一件非同尋常的事情。我把他像小孩那樣抱在懷裏，只覺得他在筆直地滑入一個深淵，而我全然無法拉住他……

他的目光很嚴肅，視線消失在很遠很遠的地方。

"我有你的綿羊。我有綿羊的箱子。還有嘴罩……"

說着，他憂鬱地微微一笑。

我等了很久。我感到他的身子漸漸暖了起來：

"小傢伙，你受驚了……"

他剛才受驚了，可不是！但他輕輕地笑了起來：

"今天晚上我要受更大的驚……"

一種無法補救的感覺，再一次使我涼到了心裏。想到從此就再也聽不到他的笑聲，我感到受不了。他的笑聲對我來說，就像沙漠中的清泉。

"小傢伙，我還想聽到你咯咯地笑……"

可是他對我説：

"到今天夜裏，就是一年了。我的星星就在我去年降落的地方頂上……"

"小傢伙，蛇啊，相約啊，星星啊，敢情只是場惡夢吧……"

可是他不回答我的問題。他對我説：

"重要的東西是看不見的……"

"可不是……"

“這就好比花兒一樣。要是你喜歡一朵花兒，而她在一顆星星上，那你夜裏看着天空，就會覺得很美。所有的星星都像開滿了花兒。”

“可不是……”

“這就好比水一樣。昨天你給我喝的水，有了那轆轤和吊繩，就像一首樂曲……你還記得吧……那水真好喝。”

“可不是……”

“夜裏，你要抬頭望着滿天的星星。我那顆實在太小了，我都沒法指給你看它在哪裏。這樣倒也好。我的星星，對你來說就是滿天星星中的一顆。所以，你會愛這滿天的星星……所有的星星都會是你的朋友。我還要給你一件禮物……”

他又笑了起來。

“呵！小傢伙，小傢伙，我喜歡聽到這笑聲！”

“這正是我的禮物……就像那水……”

“你想說甚麼？”

“人們眼裏的星星，並不是一樣的。對旅行的人來說，星星是嚮導。對有些人來說，它們只不過是天空微弱的亮光。對另一些學者來說，它們就是要探討的問題。對我那個商人來說，它們就是金子。但是所有這些星星都是靜默的。而你，你的那些星星是誰也不曾見過的……”

“你想說甚麼呢？”

"當你在夜裏望着天空時，既然我就在其中的一顆星星上面，既然我在其中一顆星星上笑着，那麼對你來説，就好像滿天的星星都在笑。只有你一個人，看見的是會笑的星星！"

説着他又笑了。

"當你感到心情平靜以後（每個人總會讓自己的心情平靜下來），你會因為認識了我而感到高興。你會永遠是我的朋友。你會想要跟我一起笑。有時候，你會心念一動，就打開窗子……你的朋友會驚奇地看到，你望着天空在笑。於是你會對他們説：'是的，我看見這些星星就會笑！'他們會以為你瘋了。我給你鬧了個惡作劇……"

説着他又笑了。

"這樣一來，我給你的彷彿不是星星，而是些會笑的小鈴鐺……"

説着他又笑了。隨後他變得很嚴肅：

"今天夜裏……你知道……你不要來。"

"我決不離開你。"

"我看上去會很痛苦……會有點像死去的樣子。就是這麼回事。你還是別看見的好，沒這必要。"

"我決不離開你。"

可是他擔心起來。

"我這麼説……也是因為蛇的緣故。你可別讓牠咬着了……蛇，都是很壞的。牠們無緣無故也會咬人……」

「我決不離開你。」

不過，他想到了甚麼，又覺得放心了：

「可也是，牠們咬第二口時，已經沒有毒液了……」

當天夜裏，我沒看見他起程。他悄悄無聲地走了。我好不容易趕上他時，他仍然執着地快步往前走。他只是對我說：

「啊！你來了……」

說完他就拉住我的手。可是他又感到不安起來：

「你不該來的。你會難過的。我看上去會像死去一樣，但那不是真的……」

我不作聲。

「你是明白的。路太遠了。我沒法帶走這副軀殼。它太沉了。」

我不作聲。

「可是這就像一棵老樹脫下的樹皮。脫下一層樹皮，是用不着傷心的……」

我不作聲。

他有點氣餒。但他重新又打起精神：

「你知道，這樣挺好。我也會望着滿天星星的。每顆星星都會有一個生鏽轆轤的水井。所有的星星都會倒水給我喝……」

我不作聲。

"這真是太有趣了！你有五億個鈴鐺，我有五億個水井……"

他也不作聲了，因為他哭了……

"到了。讓我獨自跨出一步吧。"

說着他坐了下來，因為他害怕。

他又說：

"你知道……我的花兒……我對她負有責任！她是那麼柔弱！她是那麼天真。她只有四根微不足道的刺，用來抵禦整個世界……"

我也坐下，因為我沒法再站着了。他說：

"好了……沒別的要說了……"

他稍微猶豫了一下，隨即站了起來。他往前跨出了一步，而我卻動彈不得。

只見他的腳踝邊上閃過一道黃光。片刻間他一動不動。他沒有叫喊。他像一棵樹那樣緩緩地倒下。由於是沙地，甚至都沒有一點聲響。

第二十七章

現在，當然，已經過去六年了……我還從來沒跟人講過這個故事。同伴們看見我活着回來，都很高興。我很憂傷，但我對他們説："我累了……"

現在我的心情有點平靜了。也就是説……還沒有完全平靜。而我知道，他已經回到了他的星球，因為那天天亮以後，我沒發現他的軀體。他的軀體並不太重……我喜歡在夜裏傾聽星星的聲音。它們就像五億個鈴鐺。

可是，我想到有件事出了意外。我給小王子畫的嘴罩，忘了加上皮帶！他沒法把它繫在綿羊嘴上了。於是我一直在想："在他的星球上到底會發生甚麼事呢？説不定綿羊真的吃了花兒……"

有時我對自己説："肯定不會！小王子每天夜裏給花兒蓋上玻璃罩，再説他也會仔細看好綿羊的……"於是我感到很幸福。滿天的星星輕輕地笑着。

有時我對自己說："萬一有個疏忽，那就全完了！說不定哪天晚上，他忘了蓋玻璃罩，或者綿羊在夜裏悄悄鑽了出來……"於是滿天的鈴鐺全都變成了淚珠！……

　　這可是一個很大很大的秘密喲。對於也愛着小王子的你們，就像對於我一樣，要是在我們不知道的哪個地方，有一隻我們從沒見過的綿羊，吃掉了或者沒有吃掉一朵玫瑰，整個宇宙就會完全不一樣……

　　你們望着天空，想一想：綿羊到底有沒有吃掉花兒？你們就會看到一切都變了樣……

　　而沒有一個大人懂得這有多重要啊！

　　對我來說，這是世界上最美麗、最傷感的景色。它跟前一頁上畫的是同一個景色，而我之所以再畫一遍，是為了讓你們看清這景色。就是在這裏，小王子在地球上出現，而後又消失。請仔細看看這景色，如果有一天你們到非洲沙漠去旅行，就肯定能認出它來。而要是你們有機會路過那裏，請千萬別匆匆走過，請在那顆星星下面等上一會！如果這時有個孩子向你們走來，如果他在笑，如果他的頭髮是金黃色的，如果問他而他不回答，你們一定能猜到他是誰了。那麼就請你們做件好事吧！請別讓我再這麼憂傷：趕快寫信告訴我，他又回來了……

　　　　　完